Edgar Wallace was born illegitimately in 1875 in Greenwich and adopted by George Freeman, a porter at Billingsgate fish market. At eleven, Wallace sold newspapers at Ludgate Circus and on leaving school took a job with a printer. He enlisted in the Royal West Kent Regiment, later transferring to the Medical Staff Corps, and was sent to South Africa. In 1898 he published a collection of poems called *The Mission that Failed*, left the army and became a correspondent for Reuters.

Wallace became the South African war correspondent for *The Daily Mail*. His articles were later published as *Unofficial Dispatches* and his outspokenness infuriated Kitchener, who banned him as a war correspondent until the First World War. He edited the *Rand Daily Mail*, but gambled disastrously on the South African Stock Market, returning to England to report on crimes and hanging trials. He became editor of *The Evening News*, then in 1905 founded the Tallis Press, publishing *Smithy*, a collection of soldier stories, and *Four Just Men*. At various times he worked on *The Standard*, *The Star*, *The Week-End Racing Supplement* and *The Story Journal*.

In 1917 he became a Special Constable at Lincoln's Inn and also a special interrogator for the War Office. His first marriage to Ivy Caldecott, daughter of a missionary, had ended in divorce and he married his much younger secretary, Violet King.

The Daily Mail sent Wallace to investigate atrocities in the Belgian Congo, a trip that provided material for his *Sanders of the River* books. In 1923 he became Chairman of the Press Club and in 1931 stood as a Liberal candidate at Blackpool. On being offered a scriptwriting contract at RKO, Wallace went to Hollywood. He died in 1932, on his way to work on the screenplay for *King Kong*.

D1249967

The Iron
Grip

HOUSE OF
STRATUS

This edition published in 2001 by House of Stratus, an imprint of
House of Stratus Ltd, Thirsk Industrial Park, York Road, Thirsk,
North Yorkshire, YO7 3BX, UK.

www.houseofstratus.com

Typeset by House of Stratus, printed and bound by Short Run Press Limited.

A catalogue record for this book is available from the British Library
and the Library of Congress.

ISBN 1-84232-689-9

We would like to thank the Edgar Wallace Society for all the support they have given
House of Stratus. Enquiries on how to join the Edgar Wallace Society should be addressed to:
The Edgar Wallace Society, c/o Penny Wyrd, 84 Ridgefield Road, Oxford, OX4 3DA.
Email: info@edgarwallace.org Web: http://www.edgarwallace.org/

Contents

THE MAN FROM "DOWN UNDER"

Captain Jack Bryce, inscribed in the family records as John Richard Plantagenet, but better known amongst his intimate friends as Wireless Bryce, had dropped his army title, for he had discovered that it prejudiced rather than helped his chance of securing employment. It was as plain Mr Bryce that he was ushered into the private office of Hemmer & Hemmer, and Mr James Hemmer, the senior partner of that eminent firm of lawyers, received him.

James Hemmer was an elderly man with dark, shrewd eyes, who surveyed his visitor with a brief but searching scrutiny, and seemed to Jack to be classifying him for future reference.

"Sit down, Mr Bryce," said the lawyer, taking up the card again. "You called in reference to employment, I believe?"

"Yes, sir," said Jack.

"You are not a lawyer, of course?"

Jack shook his head.

"No, sir. I am going to be perfectly frank with you. I have tried throughout the city for the past two months to get employment, but without success. I'm not suggesting that people turn me down because I'm a demobilized officer, but I do say that work is much harder to get than I ever dreamt would be the case before I left the army."

Mr Hemmer nodded sympathetically.

"I should like to help you, Mr Bryce," he said. "I knew your father well many years ago; but, candidly, the only question is your fitness for the work I have to offer. Do you understand anything about book-keeping?"

"No, sir," replied Jack, "I'm afraid I don't."

Mr Hemmer looked over the fine figure of the young man with evident approval, but he shook his head.

"It is rather terrible that a splendid specimen of a man like you cannot find employment," he said. "You stand nearly six feet, don't you?"

"Just under," smiled Jack, "and I'm fighting fit. But that doesn't help me any. I am constantly being told that brains, not brawn, is requisite; and, although I'm not a fool, I somehow haven't been able to fit myself into the jobs which have been offered me."

Mr Hemmer leant back in his chair, and shrugged his shoulders.

"I don't know what I can do, Mr Bryce," he said. "I was hoping you might take the place of one of our accountants, who is leaving us, but I think that that, you will agree, is out of the question."

Jack nodded.

"On second thoughts, I am not so sure," the lawyer went on, "that you won't be a very great help to me, providing always, of course," he added hastily, "that you do nothing illegal."

"Or, if I do anything illegal, I do it on my own responsibility," Jack amplified with a smile, which was reflected by Mr Hemmer.

"Exactly," he said. "We have a very large clientele, and we are constantly getting into difficulties from which private detectives and the ordinary resources of the law cannot extricate us. Now here is a case." He took up an envelope and extracted a letter. "Do you know Mr Dennis Wollaston by name?" Jack shook his head. "He is an extremely wealthy young man. His father was Wollaston, the big colliery proprietor, and he left his fortune equally between his daughter Grace and his son. They live in Park Lane, and our firm has acted for them for many years."

Jack waited, wondering into what difficulty the Wollastons had got, that they needed the service of his strong arm.

"Miss Wollaston is a very charming girl," continued Hemmer. "Unfortunately, her brother is not a very charming young man. And, in spite of the very respectable sum which was left him, his sister is greatly concerned as to the future of the fortune. His vice is gambling. He lost forty thousand pounds at a notorious gambling-house near Cavendish Square, and when we had that place raided he found out another. At present he seems to be frequenting the worst of all, the identity of which is at present a secret, in spite of all our efforts."

"What do you want me to do?"

"I want you to see Miss Wollaston. I met her last night at dinner, and I had a talk with her. Poor girl, she is desperate," said Mr Hemmer, shaking his head. "Not only her brother's money – but his health – is going. Undoubtedly he has got into very bad hands. She wanted me to send you to Park Lane, but I want you to meet her elsewhere, because I have an idea that one of the servants at the house is in the gambler's pay. Every time we have tried to get information, somebody has always managed to get in before us with a warning."

"What have you arranged?" asked Jack, not without interest.

Mr Hemmer took up a paper.

"You are to be in Brentford High Street, opposite the Police Court, at half-past three this afternoon. Exactly at that hour Miss Wollaston will drive up in her two-seater, and you will get into the car."

"That sounds romantic," said Jack with a bright smile, and went out in pleasant anticipation of adventure.

He had taken his stand, as he had been directed, in the narrow bottle-neck of Brentford when he saw the car approaching. It was driven by a girl of twenty-four, who was searching the sidewalk as she made her slow progress, as though seeking someone. Her eyes fell on Jack, and he lifted his hat.

"Don't trouble to stop the car," he said as he stepped on to the running-board and over the low door.

"You are Captain Bryce, aren't you?" asked the girl.

She was a wholesome, British type, tanned with the sun, and the pleasant grey eyes she bent on Jack sparkled with good humour.

"I had to choose this rather unusual method of seeing you," she said, piloting her way through the maze of traffic. "Mr Hemmer thinks that the servants are not to be trusted. I am going to drive to Hampton Court, across the bridge, and into the open country. Does that meet your views?"

"Excellently," he laughed.

She did not speak until they were clear of Hampton and had struck a secondary road, then she pulled the car to the side of the roadway and stopped the engine.

"If people see us they will take an obvious view. I hope it won't embarrass you?" she said with a laugh. Jack smiled but blushed.

"You look a capable sort of person," she went on, eyeing him with frank approval, "but I don't quite know in what capacity Mr Hemmer has sent you." She hesitated. "You're not a detective, are you?"

"No," laughed Jack. "I'm not exactly a detective. I might be more properly described as a bravo."

It was her turn to laugh.

"A hired assassin? Well, I don't want anybody assassinated, Captain Bryce, but I am very much worried about my brother. I despair of checking his excesses, and, although my best friend, Mrs Fleming – you probably know Mrs Fleming?"

"I don't go about much," said Jack, "except by motor bus."

Again she laughed.

"She has advised me to let Dennis go his own pace. Now I'll tell you my plan."

She sat back in her seat, her hands clasped about her knees, as wholesome a picture of British girlhood as Jack Bryce had ever seen.

"I have some friends in Australia, and they wrote me some months ago, telling me that a young man named Mortimer, the son of a rich squatter, was coming with a letter of introduction, and Dennis and I were going to show him round. Today I got a cable from my friends saying that he could not sail for six months, and apologizing for not having advised me sooner."

"I see," said Jack, nodding. "You would like me to be Mr Mortimer?"

"You've got it. We have promised to put him up for a day or two, and his room is quite ready. I had to see you, you know. I'm so scared about the people that lawyers employ, but you look the part."

"Prepare the blue bedroom," said Jack solemnly. "I will arrive in Park Lane at seven o'clock this evening."

At seven o'clock that night Jack, appropriately dressed in a travelling ulster, with two large portmanteaux (he had bought one that afternoon in Victoria Street) was picked up by an apologetic chauffeur, who presented his mistress' compliments and regrets for keeping him waiting. He did not see the girl when he got to the house, but when he was dressed for dinner he found her waiting in the drawing-room, and with her was a young man who sat hunched up on a settee, his hands in his pockets and a frown on his sallow face.

"Mr Mortimer? I am glad to see you," said the girl. "This is my brother Dennis."

The young man uncoiled himself from the sofa and offered a limp hand. He stood eyeing the newcomer with a certain amount of disfavour.

"How do?" he grunted ungraciously. "Is dinner ready?" – this to his sister.

Dinner was announced at that moment. Throughout the meal the young man scarcely spoke a word. Jack Bryce talked entertainingly of Australia (he had spent two hours reading an Australian novel to get the local colour), and the girl was entertained and secretly amused. Before the end of the dinner the young man got up, and with a look at his wrist-watch –

"I have an appointment. You'll excuse me, Mr Mortimer?" he said. "My sister will see you to your room. I hope you're comfortable. What is the matter?"

His sister was pulling a wry face.

"I've just remembered that I have to go to a dance," she said. "That means that poor Mr Mortimer will be left all alone in the house. I am awfully sorry."

"Don't worry about me," declared Jack cheerfully. "I can amuse myself. I know London rather well. I was here about four years ago.

But apart from that, if you give me a pack of cards I can amuse myself by playing solitaire."

There was a twisted little smile on Dennis Wollaston's face.

"Pretty slow playing against yourself, isn't it?" he asked.

"I get a lot of amusement out of it," said Jack. "I have rather a passion for cards."

"Do they play high in Australia?" asked Dennis, interested.

"Oh, pretty high," said the other carelessly. "Of course, the clubs don't allow you to lift the roof, but you can always get a little party, and in Melbourne – " He smiled suggestively, as if at a pleasant reminiscence.

The young man hesitated.

"Good night," he said. A little while later they heard the whine of his car as he drove away from the door.

The girl looked at Jack.

"Well?" she asked.

"I think he'll be easy," said that confident young man.

She was looking through the window into Park Lane. A car had drawn up at the door, and she turned to Jack.

"This is my friend, Fanny Fleming," she said. "I will introduce you."

"Not as Captain Bryce," he said quickly. "To everybody I meet here I must be Mr Mortimer."

She hesitated.

"It doesn't matter about Fanny," she began.

"It matters about everybody. You must help me if I am to help you, Miss Wollaston."

So it was as "Mr John Mortimer" that he was introduced to the slight, pretty woman of thirty who had come to take Grace Wollaston to a dance.

"You're from Australia, are you?" she asked languidly. "That is the one place I never want to go. What are you going to do with yourself in London?"

He shrugged.

"Just fool around and spend money, I expect," he said. "I am going into the country next week, but I shall be most of the time in town."

"You must get Dennis to show you round," she said with a half smile. "How did you like Dennis? I suppose you met him?"

He nodded. "Yes. A very charming man."

She smiled again.

"How diplomatic!" she said, and at that moment Grace Wollaston came in.

It was two o'clock before she returned, to find him playing patience on a little table in the drawing-room.

"Aren't you in bed?" she asked in surprise.

"No," he replied carelessly, as he gathered up the cards; "I'm waiting to see your brother."

She shook her head.

"He won't be in until four o'clock," she said, "and this is the earliest. Take my advice and go to bed, Captain Bryce. You can't do anything tonight."

"If you don't mind," he said as he rose, "I think I'll stay on."

She laughed.

"Well, you're an obstinate man. Good night."

At four o'clock that morning Mr Dennis Wollaston came home, and, seeing a light in the drawing-room, he walked in – not, it must be confessed, in the best of humours.

"What are you doing, Mr Mortimer?" he asked.

Jack had dealt two hands of five cards, and was now looking at one of them.

"I'm playing poker against myself," he said, "and I've already lost three thousand pounds."

"Have you ever lost as much as that in your life?" sneered Dennis.

"I have lost fifty thousand pounds," replied the other calmly, and Dennis looked at him with a new respect.

"That was going some," he said. "Where did this occur?"

"It occurred twice – once in Melbourne and once on the ship from Melbourne to Colombo. I got more than my losses back in

Melbourne; but I was a loser, not to the full amount, but quite enough, on the ocean trip."

Dennis seated himself and offered his cigarette case to the other.

"Do you like high play?" he asked.

"I love it," said Jack.

"You do, eh? Well, I can take you to a place where you can lose a hundred thousand pounds in a hundred minutes."

"Here in London?" said the other contemptuously. "There isn't a sport in London who'd risk a hundred thousand shillings."

"That shows what a fool you are," declared Mr Dennis Wollaston rudely. "Why, man, I've lost forty thousand pounds in this last two days."

"A straight game?"

"Of course it's a straight game," said the other indignantly. "Do you think I'm the type of man they could take in by a crooked game?"

Jack was silent.

"I'll give fifty thousand a flutter on the first opportunity."

"You can come tomorrow night," said the other quickly. "But you've got to be very careful. This is the hottest place in town. It is run by Boolby. He's a pretty well-known character, and as tough as they make them, but he's straight."

"Quite," said the other dryly.

"But you mustn't say a word to my sister, you understand. She's a fool about cards."

"Don't worry about that."

"And not a word to Mrs Fleming. I hate her, though she did me a good turn when she introduced me to Boolby's. Now meet me tomorrow at the Cridero at eleven o'clock, I'll pick you up in my car."

At eleven o'clock Jack was keeping his appointment. He had told the girl before he left the house what were his plans for the night.

Mr Dennis was not as prompt as his sister had been. It was nearly a quarter to twelve before his big, boat-like limousine swerved up to the kerb.

"Jump in quick," he said, and Jack obeyed. "I have to dodge about the town, because all sorts of detectives chase me. They know that

Boolby's running a big game, and they think that I'm one of the goats."

He drove swiftly down the Bayswater Road, and turned into a terrace of big houses. Before one of these he stopped and jumped out.

The door of the house was opened by a sedate manservant, and the two were ushered in. It looked for all the world like the abode of a middle-class household. A dim gaslight was burning in the hall; a solid mahogany hatstand and a barometer, beside a chair and a table were the only ornaments the hall contained.

Dennis led the way down a passage, and opened a small door which appeared to be a cupboard.

"Come in," he said, and Jack followed.

The door slammed, there was a rumble, and the "cupboard" started moving upwards.

"An elevator. It's the only way you can get to the top floor," chuckled Wollaston. "The stairs end at the third floor, and if you don't know the ropes you could no more get into Boolby's place than fly."

"Boolby's place" proved to be a large room, ornamented with a big, green, baize-covered table at which about fifty men and women were grouped. The game in progress was baccarat.

"I'll watch the run of the cards for a bit," said Jack.

"Let me introduce you to Boolby."

Mr Boolby was a large man, who might have been an ex-prize-fighter, an ex-butler, or an ex-gentleman. He extended a huge hand to Jack.

"Any friend of Mr Wollaston is a friend of mine," he said.

Jack turned his attention to the table, and he had not been watching long before he saw that the game was crooked. It was the dealer who betrayed the fact – the dealer who reached out to rake in the money before he had turned the cards.

It was only by a fraction of a second that he made the mistake, a mistake that escaped the observation of everybody except Jack. He looked round the table, and presently spotted the decoy duck – a tall, slim young man with whom Dennis had been exchanging friendly glances.

"I'm going to have a plunge," said this youth after the game had been in progress for an hour. "What is the bank, Jackson?"

"A hundred thousand, sir."

The youth looked at Dennis.

"I'll go banko if you'll stand half, Dennis," he said, and Dennis nodded.

"Banko," then declared the young man.

"Wait a bit," said a quiet voice.

It was Jack who spoke, and the people at the table craned round. He was smiling.

"I'll bet anybody here twenty thousand pounds that the bank's cards are two nines," he drawled; "who'll take me?"

"What the dickens do you mean?"

The big figure of Boolby elbowed a way through the press about the table.

"I mean this is a crooked game," said Jack calmly; and, stooping swiftly, he turned the cards.

As he had said, the bank's were two nines, which would beat anything.

"Every fifth, sixth, and seventh coup the bank wins," Jack went on. "And that stool pigeon" – he pointed to the slim young man – "kids somebody to come in."

By this time Boolby was facing him.

"Get out," said Boolby curtly. "Bring that lift up, Jones."

His hand was on Jack's arm, but the next instant he went down to the ground with a smashing blow in the face.

Instantly there was pandemonium. Four attendants rushed at the young man: the first he picked up and flung against the wall; the second he lifted bodily above his head; and the other two stopped in their tracks.

He took a quick glance round, then flung the man upon the green table, which collapsed with a crash under the impact, scattering cards and money in all directions.

Then he gripped Dennis by the arm.

"Come along," he said.

"What have you done!" wailed the youth. "You have acted disgracefully, you blackguard."

Jack released his arm and went back to Mr Boolby, who was sitting on the floor, his hand to his swollen jaw. He jerked the man to his feet.

"Show me the way out of this."

"I'll kill you!" hissed Boolby, and swung his arm. Again that smashing fist struck him, this time on the body, and he gasped.

"Show me the way out," repeated Jack; "or, better still, show me the way to your office."

The man was breathing heavily, and it was some time before he could speak.

"Come on," he snarled at last. "But don't forget I'll fix you for this."

They went through to another room, and through a door, down a flight of stairs, and Dennis followed. Boolby opened the door.

"Come in here," he growled.

A woman was sitting in the room, and she sprang to her feet as they entered.

"My wife. If you're a policeman, you'll know she's not in this," mumbled Boolby, but Jack was smiling at Mrs Fanny Fleming.

"So you're the real decoy duck, are you? I presume you're the person who gave away every attempt to save this boy. Come in, Wollaston."

He dragged the young man into the room, and Dennis stared from one to the other.

"Now, Boolby, you can open that safe of yours and pay over to Mr Dennis Wollaston the money he has lost since he has been your patron."

"I'll – " Boolby, spluttering with rage, could not find words to complete the sentence.

"You'll do as you're told," said Jack calmly.

"Suppose I don't?"

Jack looked round. There was a window at the end of the apartment. He walked quickly to it, pulled the blinds, opened the lower sash, and looked out.

"I guess that's far enough," he remarked. "You'll either do as I tell you, or I'll throw you out of that window. You doubt my ability?"

"Oh, pay him, pay him!" It was the white-faced Mrs Fleming who spoke. "He'll do it. I ought to have known he was a detective."

Jack was silent, but no more silent than Mr Dennis Wollaston, who seemed bereft of speech. The big man unlocked the safe and took out a bundle of notes.

"How much have you lost, you dirty little pup?" he asked.

Smack! It was the back of Jack's hand across the big man's face, and the woman shrieked.

"With men like you," said Jack, "it seems to me that only brutality counts."

Mr Boolby paid.

THE WILFUL MISS COLEBROOK

"Well, Captain Bryce, I didn't expect to send for you so soon, but I think we have another job which you can carry through for us."

Mr James Hemmer, of the firm of Hemmer & Hemmer, shook hands with the tall young man who had come into his office, and motioned him to a chair.

"Were you satisfied with the fee for the Down Under case?"

"Perfectly," replied Jack gratefully. "I really didn't expect anything like that sum, Mr Hemmer – "

Mr Hemmer stopped him with a gesture.

"It was well worth the money to get that young man out of the clutches of such scheming rascals," he said, and looked at Jack admiringly.

There was a tap at the door, and a clerk came in, and, leaning over the table, whispered to the lawyer. Mr Hemmer nodded.

"I have an appointment just now," he said, looking at Jack Bryce. "Do you mind waiting in the outer office?"

Jack Bryce made his exit and, taking the chair which the clerk put for him, waited.

When he went back to the outer office he found a frail old lady waiting, and, as she was immediately taken into Mr Hemmer's office, he gathered that she was the client who had interrupted his interview.

The door had closed, and he was speculating upon what manner of business such an old person might have to conduct when the door of the outer office was flung open violently, and a man stalked in. He was tall and broad, florid of face, perfectly dressed, and carried himself with such an air of assurance that Jack, who was quick in his likes and dislikes, marked him down unfavourably.

"Tell Mr Hemmer I am here," he said loudly to the clerk, and without so much as glancing at Jack he seated himself, opened a newspaper, and began to read.

The clerk came back from the lawyer's office and beckoned him forward, and he strode through the door and closed it behind him.

"That's a nice gentleman – I don't think," remarked the clerk, and Jack smiled.

From the inner office came the sound of the visitor's voice. It was loud and strident, and held a note of defiance. He seemed to be the only one speaking, but Jack guessed that that was because his voice was louder, and drowned all other conversation.

Presently the door of the office opened, and he flounced out, followed by the lawyer.

"I assure you, my dear Mr Benson – " began Hemmer.

"Don't dear Mr Benson me, please," said the other savagely. "I tell you that all the darned lawyers in the world, and all the darned old women in the world, will not stop me from marrying whom I choose. This is an affair which concerns Miss Colebrook and myself. She is of age, and can do as she wishes."

Mr Hemmer was obviously nettled.

"That is just what I suggest she is not doing," he retorted with asperity. "She is a foolish girl, led away by her enthusiasm. She is without experience of the world, and she has simply taken the first plausible man who has come along."

Mr Benson swung round.

"If you insult me," he shouted, "whether you're a lawyer or not a lawyer, you know what I'll do to you!"

Mr Hemmer, in spite of his self-possession, went a shade paler, and, observing this, Benson turned with a laugh, and walked out of the office, slamming the door behind him.

The lawyer stood for a little while, then, turning slowly, went back to his room and closed the door. Jack caught the clerk's smiling eye.

"We see a bit of life now and again, don't we?" commented that gentleman.

"Who is he?" asked Jack.

"Mr Larry Benson. You've heard of him?"

"I don't know him from a crow," Jack admitted.

"He's pretty well known up West," said the clerk, working as he spoke, and that seemed to summarise Mr Larry Benson's character.

Half an hour passed, and another quarter, and still the interview went on, and Jack was beginning to wonder whether Hemmer would have the opportunity of seeing him – the more so as he heard the clerk fix a telephone appointment for twelve o'clock. Then, when he had almost given up all hope, Mr Hemmer appeared in the doorway.

"Will you come in for a moment, Mr Bryce?" he said.

Jack obeyed with alacrity.

"This is Mrs Dermot." He introduced him to the old lady. "This is Mr Bryce, of whom I have been speaking."

The old lady had evidently been crying, for her eyes were red, and she looked anxiously at Jack.

"He's certainly good-looking," she said. Jack blushed.

"Mrs Dermot and I have been having a talk, Mr Bryce," Mr Hemmer explained, resuming his seat at his desk. "You probably saw the interview I had with the gentleman who left this office a few moments ago?"

Jack nodded.

"Well, I will tell you the whole story before I put any proposal to you," he went on. "Mr Larry Benson is a well-known man-about-town, though he is not so well known that I have heard anything very good of him. It has been our misfortune that he has met Mrs Dermot's niece, who is an heiress in her own right, and inherits a large sum of money next June. Miss Colebrook is a charming girl, but she has been quite carried off her feet by this" – he seemed at some loss to discover a word – "person. Now we have thought of a scheme – or, rather, I have thought of it. It is not one which I would ordinarily care to recommend to a client; but, under the circumstances, I think I am justified in putting it forward."

Mrs Dermot assented.

"Mrs Dermot and her niece are staying at a large hotel in Surrey. Mr Benson is also staying there, and every effort Mrs Dermot has made to induce her self-willed niece to leave has been unsuccessful."

Mr Hemmer paused to frame his proposal.

"We believe," he continued slowly, "that Benson has only been successful because he has never had any kind of dangerous rival, and we want to say that we honestly believe that he has only been successful at all because he has played upon the girl's imagination by representing himself as a hero. He is, as you see, a tremendous bully, and that sometimes passes for heroism to the uninitiated, and, taking the two things in conjunction, if the right kind of man is planted at Colby Hall – that is the name of the hotel – he might induce this young lady to break an engagement which can only end disastrously."

"I see," said Jack after a moment's thought. "Am I the successful rival?"

Hemmer nodded.

"I don't know whether I can play that part," said Jack doubtfully. "You see, I've had to make a rather large inroad upon my wardrobe."

Mr Hemmer smiled.

"Are your things pawned or sold?" he asked, and Jack flushed.

"They are pawned."

"That can be arranged," said the lawyer. "The question is, will you do it?"

"Yes, I'll do it," agreed Jack, again considering. "I don't want to hurt the girl, but from what I saw of the gentleman, I certainly do not regard him as an ideal husband."

The old woman rose and walked across to him, laying her hand upon his arm.

"You will be careful, young man," she said. "He has a violent temper, and is most brutal. I saw him strike a boy most cruelly because he dropped a golf club on his foot."

"He won't strike this boy most cruelly," declared Jack confidently.

That afternoon he carried the lawyer's cheque to the bank, and made divers calls at queer little shops, and the next morning a remarkably well-dressed young man, carrying two suitcases, alighted at the Ackmere Station, and entered the Colby Hall motor bus.

Mr Larry Benson was, by his own confession, a most patient man, but there was, he said, a limit to his patience. He walked gloomily along one of the garden paths – for Colby Hall was situated in the midst of a big estate – and the girl at his side was alternately angry and tearful. She was not very tall, but she was very pretty. She was the fluffy, golden type, and if her features were regular they were a trifle weak.

"I won't have it, May," said Mr Benson violently. "He's only been here three days, and yet every time I come back from town I find him with you. Who is this Captain Bryce?"

"He is very nice indeed," she said. "Now, Larry, don't be silly and jealous. You know how I love you. Tell me how you killed those seven Germans and captured their machine guns."

But Larry was in no mood for reminiscence, and was not to be smoothed down. If he had been, the sudden appearance of a tall young man in flannels who emerged from one of the side paths would have been sufficient to throw him back into his condition of smouldering fury.

Jack Bryce walked up to the girl, lifting his straw hat with a smile.

"What about that game of tennis you promised me, Miss Colebrook?"

"Miss Colebrook is not playing tennis this evening," exploded Benson, glaring at the intruder.

Jack met the glare with smiling eyes.

"Are you going to play, Miss Colebrook?"

She was in a flutter of indecision, looking from one man to the other.

"Haven't I told you," said Benson savagely, "that Miss Colebrook is not playing tennis?"

"I didn't ask you," pointed out the other with his sweetest smile.

"You asked this lady's fiancé," roared Benson, purple of face.

"What relationship you are, or hope to be, to Miss Colebrook is entirely her trouble," said Jack. "I asked her if she was playing tennis with me, and, of course, she will tell me herself. I don't know a great deal of Miss Colebrook," he added with his most winning smile, "but I doubt if she is the kind of young lady who would be bullied into breaking an engagement. You're not exactly married, Mr Benson, and, if you will allow me to say so," Jack was in his gravest and most paternal mood, "if this is the attitude you will adopt after your marriage, it is not a bright outlook for Miss Colebrook."

Benson was now speechless with rage, but the girl had plucked up a little spirit. Jack had gauged her accurately the first time he met her, and he knew just what chords to play.

"Don't be absurd, Larry!" she pouted. "Of course I'm going to play with Captain Bryce. You're very horrid and nasty." And with a toss of her head she turned and fell in by Jack's side, and they walked across to the tennis courts.

It was nearly dark before the game had finished, and Jack had seen the girl back to the hotel. On the way they passed Mrs Dermot being wheeled home in her bath-chair from her daily "constitutional." The girl was a little sad and rather thoughtful.

"I do hope I haven't hurt Larry's feelings," she said.

"Oh, nonsense!" replied Jack cheerfully. "After all, what does it matter if you have hurt his feelings?"

"Well, you see, one ought to take notice of one's future husband," she began, and Jack laughed.

"I think you're the wickedest little girl in the world," he said; and she, surprised, stared at him.

It is a painful truth that the majority of humanity are flattered by being called wicked. Miss Colebrook was no unusual specimen of humanity.

"Why do you say that?" she asked, but not resentfully.

"To play with the feelings of a man like that," said Jack admiringly. "My dear girl," he went on glibly, "you're not in love, you're just in love with love. You like nice people and nice men, but you certainly are not the type – and I think I know humanity rather well – to tie your life to Larry Benson or to any other man."

She smiled. Of course, she had never thought of her engagement to Larry Benson in any other than the most serious light, with one inevitable consequence. But she smiled.

"He's an awfully nice boy," she said with a sigh, "and so brave."

"A little on the fat side," remarked Jack critically. "I'm going to see you after dinner, aren't I?"

She dropped her eyes.

"If you like, and," hurriedly, "if Larry doesn't object."

"Forget Larry," he said.

At dinner that night Mr Larry Benson, who invariably dined with his fiancée – Mrs Dermot did not come down to dinner – left her to eat in solitary state.

"All alone?" asked Jack, entering the dining room resplendent in evening kit.

"Y-yes," replied the girl, and glanced across the tables, where a scowling Larry Benson was eating by himself.

"Fine!" observed Jack coolly, and sat down in the unoccupied chair.

He could be very amusing, for he had a fund of anecdotes which seemed inexhaustible, and there seemed to be no interval between the girl's laughter – or so it seemed to jealous Mr Benson. His mind was made up. He saw Bryce and the girl go out, and followed them.

They were walking through the darkened grounds, and Jack was spreading his overcoat on one of the garden seats, when Larry Benson overtook them.

"A word with you," he snarled.

"You can have two," said Jack.

"You can leave that lady where she is, and go back to the hotel," said Benson, "or I'll give you the biggest flogging any man has ever had in his life."

The girl came forward in alarm.

"Oh, please, don't, Larry, please!" she pleaded. But he pushed her aside so roughly that she would have fallen had not Jack caught her by the arm.

"Are you going back?" asked Benson.

"I would rather stay and be killed," Jack remarked lightly; and then, with an oath, Larry Benson struck at him.

The blow did not get home. A battering-ram caught him square under the jaw, and he fell to the ground. He jumped up, and, leaping forward, took a flying kick at his opponent. But Jack had anticipated the assault, and stepped aside. In another second a hand like a steel vice gripped Larry by the neck, another caught him by the slack of the trousers, and he found himself lifted up and flying through space. A clump of bushes broke his fall, and he lay groaning till Jack walked across to him, and, jerking him to his feet, shook him like a rat.

A deep and genuine love would probably have succoured the discomfited champion, but Jack had been very near the mark when he told her that she was only in love with love. And a feeling of this kind is rarely proof against the discovery of the unworthiness of the object that has inspired it.

The girl was watching the downfall of her mighty man of valour with wide-open mouth and staring eyes. But it was not until Mr Benson began to weep that she realized the full extent of the catastrophe, and drew the half-hoop of diamonds from her finger with becoming dignity.

"Mr Benson," she said, "here is your ring."

He took the ring, because Mr Benson was a man who never left any of his property in other people's possession if he could help it.

"And I want to say this," declared the girl, "that I don't believe you ever did kill seven Germans with your own hand – or even six."

They watched him stagger away, and then – "Sit down with me, little friend," said Bryce, "and let's talk about love."

"Yes, auntie," said May Colebrook next morning, and she was quite brisk and business-like, "I've broken off my engagement with Mr Benson. I don't think he's the type of man that one could respect. You may think I'm romantic, but I must have a man I respect."

"Yes, my dear," agreed the meek Mrs Dermot.

"I had a long talk with Mr Bryce last night, and he really is a sensible man, and I'm awfully sorry he's gone away this morning," she said. "You know, I was never in love at all, I was merely in love with love. That's quite a different thing. And I've got too many responsibilities in this world to marry in haste. If one has a lot of money, one ought to take the greatest care that it doesn't fall into hands which might employ it for evil."

Mrs Dermot was staggered, and quite justifiably so, for she had never heard her niece talk in this strain before.

"I think you're very sensible, May," she remarked. "When did you reach this conclusion?"

"Oh, I've been thinking matters out," said her niece.

But she did not say that she had been thinking matters out with Jack Bryce, and that the admirable sentiments which she enunciated were merely echoes of his.

THE TYRANT OF THE HOUSE

Jack Bryce was taking a little gentle exercise in his Bloomsbury apartment after breakfast. He was stripped to the waist, and his magnificent torso showed the play of his back muscles, for his "gentle exercise" consisted of lifting the sofa on the palm of the one hand and transferring it over his head to the palm of the other.

In the midst of this amusement the telephone bell rang, and he put the sofa down so gently that no sound was heard in the room below.

The house had been in the occupation of the military during the war, and this unusual telephone service was the result.

It was Hemmer on the telephone.

"Are you at home, Mr Bryce?"

"Yes, sir," said Jack. "Would you like me to come up?"

"No, thank you. I'm on my way to Bloomsbury to consult some solicitors who are acting in conjunction with us, and I will call, if it is convenient."

Half an hour later Mr Hemmer was shown into Jack's room.

"You have a nice apartment, Mr Bryce," he said. "I'm happy to think that things are going so well with you."

"I've had the most amazing luck," agreed Jack. "But the biggest bit of luck was drifting into your office that morning in the hope of getting an odd job. Have you something for me?"

Mr Hemmer had taken a seat and was opening his black bag.

"I have," he said; "but it isn't going to be a tremendously remunerative job."

"That doesn't worry me," smiled Jack Bryce.

"Ah, here are the notes I have made," said Mr Hemmer, taking out a sheet of paper.

He adjusted his glasses and glanced over his paper. Then he took off his glasses, put the notes back in his bag, and smiled at Jack.

"A very old and valued client of mine," he began, "Mrs Cartwright, was left a widow some six years ago with very considerable property. She had one child, a girl, Jean, and the lady might have had a very comfortable time indeed if she hadn't met with the most unmitigated tyrant that it has been my lot to meet. This man she married. No; I don't think he was after her money; he has property of his own, and how she came to marry him at all is a mystery to me, although, in spite of her fifty years, she is still a very attractive woman."

Jack nodded. These stories of human people fascinated him; and, did the lawyer but know it, he lived in daily terror of losing his connection with the firm of Hemmer and Hemmer – not so much for the money which his work brought in (and he already had a snug balance in the bank), but for the extraordinary experiences they procured.

"I might tell you that Miss Jean Cartwright is Miss Jean Wilson – that was her father's name, though Jean, whom I have known since she was a baby, adopted the name of Cartwright in order to save trouble at home. Cartwright, as I say, is a domestic tyrant of the most virulent type. Although she has only been married a little over two years, poor Mrs Cartwright bitterly repents her bargain, but she is too timid and nervous a woman to stand up for herself. Last week she consulted me as to a judicial separation – a step which she is loth to take, mainly, I think, because she is afraid of her husband. It was then that I thought of you, and suggested to Mrs Cartwright a plan which she hesitated to adopt, but which Jean, who is ever so much more strong-minded, has insisted upon."

"What is the plan?" asked Jack when the lawyer paused.

"I suggested to her that she should spring a son upon her husband."

"A son!" gasped Jack.

"Yes," nodded the lawyer. "There is no reason why she shouldn't have had a son who went to Canada as a boy. At any rate, we've prevailed upon the lady to take this step, and in great fear and trembling she told her husband one morning at breakfast – which doesn't seem the most tactful moment to have chosen – that she had a son in Canada who was coming home. Of course, he was furious, raved and fumed, and said that she had deceived him; demanded why she had kept her secret so long, and then, I'm afraid – " the lawyer smiled mischievously, "she had to give you rather a bad character."

· "I know," nodded Jack. "I was the bad egg that they could do nothing with and ran away to sea."

"Exactly," said Mr Hemmer. "Well, what do you think of it?"

"When do I arrive from Canada? If I remember rightly, last time I arrived from Australia."

"You arrive from Canada on Wednesday morning. Your sister will come and meet you at Euston Station. She will wear a long white coat, and will carry a green handbag. Do you think you will miss her?"

"I'm just as likely to miss Euston," said Jack cheerfully.

He took his trunks and his travelling coat to Euston half-an-hour before it had been arranged he should be called for, and exactly at three o'clock he saw, walking up and down the station – at the end of one of the platforms – a slim figure in a white coat, carrying a vivid green handbag. He went up to her, and she turned, looked at him in amazement and burst into a fit of uncontrollable laughter.

"Poor mother will have a fit when she sees you," she said as he took her hand. "What a big fellow you are! The Wilsons are all small."

"It is the climate of Canada," said Jack calmly.

"You'll have to meet mother first," she said. "We stayed overnight at Aunt Martha's house – Auntie is out of town – so it is very convenient for all concerned."

On the way to the aunt's house she gave a brief and not too flattering sketch of her stepfather.

"He is a most terrible bully," she said, "and treats mother abominably. I would have left the house only I can't leave poor mother alone and at his mercy."

"What do you mean by treating her abominably?" asked Jack. "Does he strike her?"

"No," said the girl, shaking her head, "but he just stops short of that. He keeps her in a condition of dread and nervousness all the time. Meal times are positively dreadful."

"In appearance what is he like?"

"He is rather a big man, but not so tall as you. He has a stiff little black beard and rather a red face and he is terribly strong, so please don't fall foul of him."

"Terribly strong, is he?" smiled Jack. "He must have been talking about himself."

His new "mother" greeted him with consternation.

"Oh, he'll never believe you're my son," she wailed in despair. "Darling, don't you think it would be better if we pretended that he hadn't come after all?"

"No, mother," said the girl firmly. "You've got to get used to Jack – that is your name, isn't it? And you've got to get used to his kissing you and saying good night."

Mrs Cartwright was still a pretty woman, and she flushed.

"I've got used to worse things than that, my dear," she said grimly. "And I suppose you'll have to submit to something of the same yourself?"

"Me?" said the girl in alarm. "Brothers and sisters don't kiss. What do you think, Mr Bryce?"

"It is a matter for you to settle yourself," said Jack primly. "But I only want to warn you that kissing is an extra, and will be charged for on the bill." And they laughed together, and in their laughter came nearer to a common understanding.

Mr Cartwright had not come back from the City when they arrived at Chiselhurst, and Jack went to his room. The Cartwrights did not dress for dinner, and Jack employed the hour of waiting in sitting in a window-seat in his bedroom and watching the front porch and the pathway leading thereto. Presently he saw a man walking up the drive with brisk steps.

"That's the lad, is it?" said Jack to himself.

Mr Cartwright might be a formidable antagonist, for he was tall, broad and sturdy-looking. But Jack Bryce knew something of men, and had Mr Cartwright been as tall as a house he would have had no doubt in his mind of the outcome of any struggle.

He had a brief interview with the girl before he went in to dinner.

"You must tell your mother not to be surprised at anything I do. Remember, I'm the bad egg of the family."

She nodded, and there was dancing laughter in her eyes.

Jack went in to dinner, and found the owner of the house with his back to the fire, his hands behind him. He scowled at Jack as he came in.

"William, this is my son, Jack," said Mrs Cartwright timidly.

"Oh it is, is it?" said the amiable William, and made no attempt to offer his hand. "Is dinner ready, because I'm hungry? This house is run like a barn," he stormed. "I told you that I wanted dinner at seven o'clock, and it is now five minutes past."

"In a moment, dear," fluttered Mrs Cartwright. "The cook has had toothache."

"Damn the cook and her toothache!" roared Cartwright.

He was saved any further expression of his views by the arrival of the joint. He took up his carving-knife and began to slice the beef. It was undoubtedly tough; from where he sat Jack could see that much. But it was not tough enough to justify Mr Cartwright's subsequent action. With an oath he picked up the dish and flung it, meat and all, into the hearth.

"Bring me some cold meat," he said, and dodged his head just in time.

A plate went spinning past him and fell with a crash in the grate. He stared across at Jack.

"Pick up that meat," yelled Jack, and his face was so demoniacal that even the girl was deceived.

"What – what?" spluttered Mr Cartwright.

"Pick it up!" And again the bearded man had to dodge the plate that went spinning past his ear. "Pick it up, you great lump of flesh!" roared Jack.

Cartwright rose mechanically, went to the hearth and looked down.

"Where shall I put it?" he asked.

"Put it on a plate. Here's one. Catch!"

Again a plate flew towards him, and with more luck than judgment he caught it in his fumbling grasp, lifted the joint from the fender, and put it upon the plate.

"Now take it out to the kitchen and wash it. And don't keep me waiting for my dinner, or I'll beat your pin-head as flat as a nickel!" said Jack pleasantly. And like a man in a trance Mr Cartwright walked out.

His wife was pale and speechless. Jean, her pretty face red with suppressed laughter, waited until the door closed behind her stepfather, then leaned back in her chair and shrieked her merriment.

"He'll hear you, my dear."

"Let him," said Jack.

The older woman looked at him pleadingly.

"He will be terribly angry when he comes back, Mr – I mean, Jack. Do you think you ought to stay?"

"Stay?" Jack laughed. "The only question which is agitating the mind of your husband is, how long *he* is going to stay? Here he comes."

Evidently Mr Cartwright had recovered some of his fine animal spirits, for he flounced in, almost threw the joint upon the table, and glared across the table at Jack.

"Now, sir," he said, "perhaps you will explain your extraordinary conduct."

Jack looked round the table with so fiendish an expression that even the girl winced. Presently he saw what he was looking for – a bread-knife – and, leaning across, he grabbed it.

"What did you say?" he asked in a hollow voice.

Mr Cartwright's face was white.

"I – I – was saying – don't you think you are being very hasty?" he stammered.

"Carve up that meat," said Jack deliberately. "I'll talk to you after dinner, my lad – when my mother and sister are out of sight and hearing," he added significantly.

And then he did an old trick of his, and one which had amused many a mess in his old army days. He took up a fork from the table and absent-mindedly twisted it round his finger as though it were made of lead. Mr Cartwright stared and gasped. Mrs Cartwright sat open-mouthed, and only the girl maintained her poise.

"Great heavens! You must be strong!" she said admiringly.

"What's that?" said Jack with a start, and looked down at his finger. "I'm awfully sorry, I've spoilt your fork."

He gripped the ends, and with apparently no effort straightened the fork out again, though the girl could see the ripple and play of his biceps under his close-fitting coat.

Mr Cartwright said not a word. He walked slowly round the table, picked up the fork and tried to bend it with both hands. It yielded a little, but only a little. He put the fork back on the table, resumed his seat, and did not speak throughout the meal.

When dinner was at an end and the ladies rose, he looked apprehensively at his wife.

"Don't you think you'd better stay a little longer, dear? I'd like to hear something of your son's adventures in Canada."

"I can tell you those alone," said Jack.

The man sat uneasily in his chair, eyeing his "stepson," and when the door closed behind the ladies he put his hand in his pocket.

"Have a cigar, Jack, my boy," he said, and Jack took the cigar, smelt it, bit off the end and struck a match.

"How long are you staying with your mother?" asked Mr Cartwright carelessly.

"About two years," said Jack, puffing at his smoke, and he grinned inwardly as he heard Mr Cartwright's ill-suppressed groan.

Presently:

"Are you staying *here*?" he asked with an effort, and emphasized the last word.

Jack nodded.

"You and I will get on all right, Mr Cartwright," he said. "You must excuse my little outbursts of temper. But the fact is, I got sunstroke when I was in the Rocky Mountains, and I've never quite been the same since. I've been very lucky," he added thoughtfully. "When I killed that fellow in Edmonton – "

"Killed a fellow in Edmonton!" said Mr Cartwright in a quavering voice. "I never heard of that. What had he done?"

"I didn't like the look of his face, poor fellow!" said Jack carelessly. "But then, I was much more particular in those days than I am now," and he looked suggestively at Mr Cartwright.

"Did you – shoot him?"

"No – strangled him," said Jack. "I don't believe in shooting people."

Cartwright looked at the other's hands and shuddered.

"Is that the only man you've killed?" he asked, swallowing hard.

"There was another one," said Jack moodily; "but I don't like to talk about him. I should never have done it, but for the fact that I was in drink. Drink makes me a raving lunatic. Have you any wine in the house, by the way?" he asked.

"*No!*" said Mr Cartwright loudly and promptly.

"Perhaps I have a flask in my case," said Jack, half rising from his chair.

"Don't, don't," cried Mr Cartwright. "Have tea, my boy, it's the finest thing in the world for calming the savage breast. Ha, ha!"

There was no amusement in his laughter.

"I'm very glad to see this evening has passed off as well as it has," said Jack. "You see, the thing was so unexpected, your throwing the food in the fire and all that sort of thing, that I was quite taken aback. I've been sitting here wondering whether I am a changed man. I must be." He shook his head wonderingly. "The mere fact that you are sitting here alive, and that I'm not in gaol, proves to me that a change has come over my spirit."

"I hope so," said Cartwright faintly.

"Perhaps it hasn't," said Jack thoughtfully. "However, we will see another time."

Mr Cartwright resolved most fervently that there would be no other time.

They went into the drawing-room, where the women were, and Mr Cartwright seemed something like the old Mr Cartwright his wife had known in his brief courting days. In truth he was the type of man who is spoilt by the submission of weaker people than himself. There are such men, who must either be tyrannized or be tyrants; and Cartwright was an excellent specimen of this type. He was not to forgo his fight for supremacy, however, and a night's sleep did wonders towards the restoration of the old Adam.

Jack heard his loud and bullying voice shouting down the stairs. He heard him spluttering up and down the passage, calling for his boots. He heard Mrs Cartwright's agitated attempts to soothe her angry lord. And he swung his legs over the bed, put his feet into his slippers, and got into his dressing-gown.

"This is not a house, it's a lunatic asylum," Mr Cartwright was roaring as Jack came into the passage.

The girl, who was standing at her door, saw a tall, dishevelled young man come blinking into the light.

"Where's my gun, Johnson?" he asked hoarsely, and Mr Cartwright's eloquence was arrested.

"What is it, old man? There's no Johnson here; you're asleep."

"Where's my gun, Johnson?" demanded Jack in an awful voice. "There's an Indian with a black beard, and I've sworn that I'll wipe him out. Look in my portmanteau, somebody. I want the long one with the pearl handle."

"Send for a doctor," said Mr Cartwright, and then Jack came out of his trance.

He explained at breakfast that if he was awakened by a loud noise in the morning, he invariably lost his head. He thought it was the result of his being struck by lightning in Manitoba.

"You've been struck by lightning and had sunstroke," said Mr Cartwright thoughtfully. "Has anything else happened to you?"

"I once fell over a cliff in my sleep," said Jack modestly. "You see, some nights, when I'm not feeling good, I get kind of haunted with the ghosts of the men I have killed. Of course, it's all absurd, and there are no such things as ghosts; but occasionally I get up in the middle of the night, about one o'clock. But I'm perfectly harmless, and I believe I know what I'm doing, because I have never shot anybody yet – not in my sleep, I mean."

He looked at Mr Cartwright profoundly.

"Not yet," he added, and Mr Cartwright breathed quickly.

Three days Jack stayed at Chiselhurst, and matters went smoothly. On the third night Jean said:

"I think you've got him tamed. I wish to heaven you could make him run away," said the girl. "Mother's looking quite well, isn't she?"

Jack shook his head.

"I don't think he's tamed. In fact, he has been so infernally polite today that I rather fancy he is saving something up for me."

What that something was, he was to learn. Mr Cartwright came home with a guest, a man ill at ease, in brand-new clothes, who spoke very little but looked a lot. And Mr Cartwright's manner had undergone a change. He had suddenly assumed the old hectoring, bullying tone, roared at the servants, at his wife, at the girl; and when Jack spoke gently to him, he snapped back. All the time, as Jack did not fail to observe, the guest, who had been introduced as Mr Smith, kept his beady eyes on Jack.

"So that's it," thought the strong-arm man with inward joy. "He has brought a bruiser home to tame *me!*"

The girl leant over the table and spoke to him in a low tone.

"I don't understand this, Jack," she said. "That man is fearfully common – not the type that Mr Cartwright would ordinarily bring to dinner. Who is he?"

"I think he's a prize-fighter," said Jack in the same tone.

"What the devil are you whispering about?" shouted Mr Cartwright. "I'll have no whispering at my table."

Jack's hand moved so quickly that even the watchful guest could not stop the act. There had been a plate with a solid-looking blancmange before Jack, and now the plate was empty – the blancmange was spread over Mr Cartwright's large face.

"Here, none of that."

It was the guest who spoke, and he leapt up, overturning his chair, and gripped the strong man's arm. And then into his face there crept a look of surprise and fear.

"Let go," he snarled.

The women had risen and were staring, horrified, at the unexpected development. Only Mr Cartwright stood, his hands in his pockets, his legs wide apart, beaming upon his protégé.

"Give it him!" he said.

"Let go," gasped the man, and struck out wildly, hitting nothing but the air.

Then with a jerk he was lifted from his feet, flung through the window – curtain, blind, window-box – and fell in a heap in the garden outside, enveloped and covered with the debris he had carried with him.

"You're going that route, too, Cartwright," said Jack with a fiendish grin.

"For God's sake don't touch me! I've a weak heart," fluttered Cartwright.

"I'm going up to my room to get my riding-crop, and you're due for the biggest flogging that any man ever had," said Jack, repeating the words of one who had uttered the same threat, but with disastrous results to the threatener. "Just wait here till I come down."

Mr Cartwright waited only just so long as it took Jack to mount the stairs. When the sound of his feet came from the room overhead, Mr Cartwright darted out of the room, grabbed his hat from the hall-stand and bolted.

A fortnight later Jack met Mr Hemmer in Chancery Lane.

"You'll be interested to know, Captain Bryce," said that worthy man, "that Cartwright has expressed his willingness to be sued for a divorce."

"On what grounds?" asked Jack in surprise.

"On the grounds of incompatibility of temperament and desertion," said the lawyer.

"Isn't he going back to his wife?"

"Not if he knows it," said the lawyer emphatically; "and I gather that he does know it!"

THE KIDNAPPED TYPIST

Jack Bryce surveyed the world from the top of a motor omnibus, and found it good. He was on his way to meet Mr Hemmer, of Hemmer & Hemmer's, and the place appointed was an unusual one. Moreover, it did not seem that the business would develop in such a manner as would greatly benefit him in his new career. But Hemmer had telephoned his orders, and he whistled cheerfully as he descended from the bus at the narrow entrance of Little Thames Lane.

He made his way along the narrow thoroughfare till he came to a door above which were the words, in faded green letters – "Letitsky, merchant."

He walked into the dirty hallway, which terminated in a lift opening, and passed through a door marked "Office" on his left. There was a counter, behind which was a pale-faced little man, who seemed extraordinarily agitated. He was on the point of going out of the second door when Jack entered, and turned round with a nervous start.

"What do you want?" he asked with a foreign accent.

"A friend of mine told me to meet him here," said Jack. "Mr – "

"We don't know anything about your friends – you can't stay here!" almost screeched the little man, and bolted through the door.

Jack stared after him with a grin. He had not come all the way to the City to be so summarily dismissed. He seated himself on the one chair which the office boasted. From behind the glass partition he heard voices raised, and gathered that he had really arrived at a very inopportune moment.

"You will do as I tell you," said a harsh voice. "And if you are a sensible girl…"

He did not hear the remainder. Presently a girl's voice, wrathful and agitated, came to him:

"I won't – I won't… You have no right to expect me to… I have telephoned to my uncle's solicitor…"

Jack paid a little more attention at this.

"You fool!" growled the man's voice savagely.

"I don't care what you say," said the girl. "I'm not going to be mixed up in – "

And here her voice was abruptly terminated, and Jack had a suspicion that somebody had put a hand in front of her mouth. He frowned. He did not want to interfere in what might be a purely private and a very intimate quarrel, and yet the thought that violence was being done to some woman, even though that woman were the wife of the proprietor, gave him an uncomfortable twinge.

It seemed to Jack that there was a little scuffle in the inner office, and his hand was again on the flap when the little white-faced man came back, more agitated than ever.

"Here, where are you going?" he asked in alarm.

"What is the trouble?" demanded Jack.

"No business of yours," said the other quaveringly. "You get out. Mr Letitsky doesn't want you here."

Jack did not move, eyeing the other thoughtfully.

"What is the game?" he asked again. "Don't tell me it's amateur theatricals, because I've heard that stuff before."

"If you don't go I'll send for the police," shrilled the little fellow, and his English became more and more shaky. "Have I to tell you more as once to get out? Suppose I send for the police, eh?"

"All right," said Jack easily. "Send for the police. But still you haven't satisfied me as to what the trouble is."

At that moment the outer door opened, and Hemmer came in from the street. He did no more than nod to Jack.

"Well?" asked the little man loudly.

"I am Mr Hemmer," said that gentleman, "of the firm of Hemmer & Hemmer, solicitors. You probably know my name."

"Yes, sir," replied the other more respectfully.

"I have come to see Miss Skinner. She telephoned to me half an hour ago."

"Miss Skinner is out," said the man loudly.

"Out!" exclaimed Mr Hemmer in surprise. "When do you expect her back?"

"She won't be back today," said the man, who seemed to be growing more and more agitated.

"Humph!" said the lawyer with a frown. "She asked me particularly to come at once – "

"She's gone out, I tell you, and she's not coming back today. In fact, the boss has fired her for cheeking him."

"I see," said the lawyer, and turned to go. Jack followed him out. They were stopped a moment by a porter, who was carrying in a heavy bale of cloth, which slipped as he came opposite the lawyer, and fell with a thud to the ground. The man cursed and called out to his fellows, who were standing on the sidewalk unloading a heavy van.

"Come on, a couple of you," he said. "Help me up with this bale; I've dropped it."

"Excuse me," said Jack, and, stooping down, lifted the bale with apparently no effort, and placed it on the astonished man's shoulders.

The lawyer stared at him in amazement.

"My friend," he said, "I didn't realize you were so strong. I can't make this business out, Bryce. Why should the girl go out?"

"I'm positively certain she has not left the building," declared Jack.

And he told the lawyer what he had overheard.

Mr Hemmer looked at him suspiciously and stroked his chin.

"It is very curious," he said; "most curious." He hesitated. "Letitsky's have not the best of names in the City, and, to be perfectly frank, I do not like this business."

He walked by Jack's side into the crowded main street, where his car was waiting.

"I asked you to meet me here because I am going out of town at one o'clock, and I couldn't see you at any other time, and I wanted to send you to see another client of mine, but she can wait," he said. "This business is too strange for me. Miss Skinner is the niece of a valued client of ours, and I warned him not to allow her to go into this office."

"Have they a bad reputation?" asked Jack.

"No," hesitated the lawyer; "it isn't that. But they're shaky and tricky. They've been on the verge of bankruptcy two or three times, and they were concerned in some particularly unpleasant contract scandal during the war. My client lives in Cheshire, and I promised to keep an eye on the young lady, and that, I suppose, is the reason she's called me up."

He shook his head.

"I don't like it," he remarked.

"I'm sure she's in the building," said Jack.

The lawyer bit his lip in thought.

"Would you be good enough to keep an eye on these premises?" he asked. "And if you see Miss Skinner – she is rather a good-looking girl of middle height – I wish you'd intercept her, either going in or coming out, and tell her to come to my office."

Jack nodded.

"Nothing will give me greater pleasure, particularly if it leads to a rough house with that worm behind the counter," he said.

The lawyer drove off, and Jack walked slowly down the street. The hours passed, but there was no sign of Grace Skinner (Grace was her Christian name, he had discovered from the lawyer).

Two o'clock – three o'clock – four o'clock; and as the latter hour was striking, two disreputable-looking men passed into the doorway of Letitsky's, and almost immediately afterwards the little white-faced man came out, hatless, and walked quickly into Cheape Street.

He did not notice Jack, who kept himself as much in the background as possible. Presently the little man came back, and this time he was riding in a taxicab, which he left at the door, disappearing into the interior. Jack strolled across the street. The taxi-driver was a good-natured looking burly man who nodded as Jack came up.

"Very sorry, sir, I'm engaged," he said, "worse luck!"

"Why worse luck?" asked Jack.

"Well, who wants to go to Stortford, thirty miles from London?" he said. "But it's a police job, so I can't help myself."

"A police job, eh?" remarked Jack thoughtfully, and as he spoke the two men came out, and between them a pale, pretty girl.

Jack gasped at the sight of her, because she was handcuffed, and the men were holding her by the arms. They were hurrying her into the cab when he pushed aside one of her custodians, and asked:

"Are you Miss Skinner?"

"Here, what do you want?" demanded the man whom he had pushed aside. "I'm a detective, and I'm arresting this woman on a charge of theft and slander."

"It isn't true," cried the girl. "I have never stolen anything. Oh, it's wicked, wicked!"

"But," said Jack in astonishment, "are you being arrested?"

The girl nodded.

"Because I said – "

"Put her in the cab. What the dickens are you waiting for?" It was a voice from the doorway that spoke, and Jack saw a big, stout man, whose high cheekbones and Slavonic cast of countenance marked him as Paul Letitsky.

"Why is this lady being arrested?" he demanded.

"What business is that of yours? Ask the police," snarled the other.

Jack was in a dilemma. The girl had admitted the arrest, and he hesitated to interfere.

"Why is she being taken to Stortford?"

The man's face went livid.

"It's because the crime was committed at Stortford," he said, "and she will be charged there."

By this time the girl had been pushed into the cab, and the two men had followed, slamming the door behind them. As the taxi moved off, leaving Jack on the sidewalk, Letitsky beckoned him.

"Come in here," he said, and Jack followed into the outer office. "Now, you're a smart fellow," pursued the stout man, "and you don't want to give us any trouble, I'm sure."

"I'm not so certain about that," said Jack. "Under certain circumstances I would give you a lot of trouble."

"You're a private detective, I suppose? Well, I'll tell you what I'll do. I'll give you £50 to go away and forget – how will that suit you?"

The fat man peered earnestly into his face.

"It doesn't suit me at all," replied Jack, "until I know exactly why this lady has been arrested, and just why you are trying to bribe me to keep my mouth shut about it."

"I am not trying to bribe you," roared the man. "Go out of this, and do as you darned well please! Go on, out you go!"

In his mistaken zeal, he gripped Jack by the arm and pushed him towards the door. The next instant the tall man had turned, and, lifting the other as easily as though he were a child, had seated him on the table, as you might seat a small boy. A few seconds later Jack was on his way to Stortford.

His car broke down, however, fifteen miles from Stortford, and as he could not get another, and had to train, it was not until eight o'clock that night that he reached his destination.

"Mr Letitsky?" said the railway porter. "Oh, yes; he's got a house up on Summer's Hill. If you take the station fly it'll get you up there in a quarter of an hour."

"No, thanks," replied Jack. "I'll walk."

It was a big house, this residence of the merchant, and was surrounded by a high wall. Jack was on the point of scaling it when he remembered that he had not made one elementary inquiry which was very necessary. He was so certain that the theory he had worked out that afternoon was correct that he had not troubled to call at the police station. For his own protection, however, he must tramp back to the little village, and waste a valuable hour or two.

The police station at Stortford was a small cottage with a lock-up at the back. The sergeant in charge was at first not inclined to be communicative.

"No," he said, "we've no prisoners from London. Are you expecting a friend of yours?" he asked sarcastically.

"My Aunt Jane," replied Jack; and then, satisfied, he walked back to the house, and was making his preparations to climb the wall when a boy on a bicycle came hurriedly along the dark road, and, dismounting before the iron gates, rang a bell.

There was evidently some sort of lodgekeeper, for Jack heard the creak of bolts almost immediately. He crept nearer and saw, despite the darkness, that the newcomer was a telegraph boy, and, like most country telegraph boys, he was talkative.

"Here you are, Jim," he said; "there's a telegram for Mr Letitsky. It's bad news, too."

"What is it?" growled the lodgekeeper.

"His store is burnt down."

Jack waited to hear no more. Abandoning all idea of climbing the wall he stepped suddenly from the darkness before the astounded lodgekeeper, and pushed his way through the gates.

"Where are you going?" asked the man.

"I'm going to see Letitsky, that's all," said Jack, and walked rapidly up the drive.

The man came after him at a run and grabbed him. But Jack Bryce was in a hurry. He lifted the lodgekeeper as if he had been a sack of feathers and tossed him into a bush.

His ring at the door was immediately answered, and again he brushed past the footman and turned into a room at the right, where he had seen a light.

Mr Letitsky was smoking a large cigar, and with him was the pale-faced man whom Jack had interviewed earlier in the day. At the sight of the intruder Letitsky sprang to his feet with an oath.

"What do you want?" he demanded, white as death.

"I want Miss Grace Skinner, who is a prisoner in this house," said Jack. "And afterwards I shall want you."

"Who are you?" spluttered Letitsky.

"You ought to guess," said Jack.

"My God! From Scotland Yard?" gasped the alien.

At this word the little man made an attempt to dart past Jack into the hall, and was gripped by the collar, shaken like a rat, and firmly deposited on a sofa.

"Now, where's Miss Skinner?"

"I'll show you; I'll show you," squeaked the little man. "I'm not in this, sir; really I'm not! Letitsky brought me into it. Let me show you, sir!"

He raced up the stairs, and Jack followed, leaving Letitsky to his own devices. On the third floor the man paused before a door and flung it open. The girl, sitting on the edge of the bed, rose in alarm as Jack entered.

"It's all right, Miss Skinner," said Jack with a smile. "I'm from your lawyer, and have come to take you home."

"Oh, thank God!" sobbed the girl, and would have fallen if Jack had not caught her.

There was the sound of a shot, and Jack looked round.

"What was that?" whispered the frightened girl.

"Nothing," said Jack reassuringly.

Nevertheless, he led the girl past the open door of the drawing-room, where Letitsky lay dead upon the floor, a smoking revolver in his hand.

"I knew, of course, that the firm of Letitsky's was shaky," the girl explained later to Jack and Mr Hemmer, "and that they were hard put to it to find money, but I had no idea that they were in such a desperate state that they were going to burn down the warehouse. Yet that must have been their plan, for I know that the warehouse was very heavily insured, and Mr Letitsky mentioned casually that maybe I could take a holiday next week," said the girl.

"Today I happened to go into the cellar where the office supplies are stored, and found tins of petrol and a time machine. I didn't know what it was till I came back and asked Mr Letitsky, and then he fell into such a state of rage that I guessed. He wanted me to swear that I would say nothing, and offered me a thousand pounds; and then, when I wouldn't fall in with his plans, he locked me up in one of the inner offices, and said he'd kill me if I made a sound. He told me when be got me here that he was taking me to the Continent, and that I should have to marry him, because a wife could not give evidence against her husband."

Jack nodded.

"The detectives, of course, were fellows in the pay of Letitsky," he said.

Afterwards, when the girl had gone, Mr Hemmer took a paper from his pocket, and handed it to Jack.

"A little cheque, Captain Bryce," he said. "I dare say the insurance company will supplement this reward. Incidentally," he said, "I think I shall have one or two other jobs which will be greatly to your liking."

THE VLAKFONTAIN DIAMOND

It was ten o'clock on a foggy November night, and Jack Bryce was literally groping his way to his Bloomsbury lodgings, and had, in fact, reached the street where he lived, when out of the gloom approached two strangers. It was too dark to see their faces, but from their hang-dog carriage he mentally classified them as members of that strange underworld of London which is peopled alike by the mendicant and the crook, who differ very little in appearance.

"Excuse me, guv'nor," said one of the men, "is your name Bryce?"

Jack raised his eyebrows in surprise, for he had the impression that they had come upon him by the veriest accident. And then he remembered that he was only a few doors from his house, and must of necessity come the way he was coming if his afternoon business were known, so that there was nothing mysterious in the question.

"My name is Bryce," he replied.

He had hardly spoken the words when the first of the two men was on him with a knobbly stick, which was ominously thin, and which he diagnosed rightly as being a piece of gaspipe. He slipped nimbly to the left, and the weapon fell with a thud against the railings by which he was standing. He was not so fortunate in dodging the blow from the second man, which caught his shoulder, and for a moment numbed him, but one of his arms was in working order, and of this he made good use.

The first of his attackers he caught with a smashing blow under the jaw, the second he gripped by the collar, and with no effort tossed him over the railings into the area below. He heard the crash of the body as it struck the ground, then stooped and jerked the first man to his feet.

"My friend," he said between his teeth, "I think you're going to tell me just why this business happened."

There was a loud groan from the area below.

"Go down and pick up your pal," ordered Jack. "Wait a minute."

He passed his hands deftly over the man's clothes, but there was no other weapon. Evidently the man who had taken that fearful fall had been lucky, for he was able to rise with the assistance of his friend and climb the area steps.

"Hurt?" asked Jack laconically, and the man growled something. "No bones broken at any rate," remarked Jack. "I think, my friend, you were born to be hung. Now, both of you lads can come with me to the nearest lamp-post. I want to have a look at you, and afterwards you're going to tell me just why you prepared this pleasant little welcome home for me."

He gripped them, one by each arm, and dragged them forward to the light. Under the rays of the big arc-lamp he could see them plainly, despite the fog.

"Now," he demanded, "who put you up to this?"

"A toff," growled one. "It's not our job, guv'nor, but this toff came down to the East End for us, and told us there was a man he wanted to beat up."

"What was his name?"

"You don't suppose he gave us his name, do you?" snarled the other.

"Where were you supposed to report?" asked Jack, and the man was silent, and then Bryce gripped him by the neck, and he yelled:

"I tell you, I don't know! Never saw him before in my life!"

His words carried conviction to Jack Bryce, and after a second of thought he twisted the man round.

"Goodbye and godspeed!" he said, and literally kicked him into the fog.

The other, who had had the fall, was rubbing his elbows and his knees, keeping an apprehensive eye upon his custodian.

"You ain't 'arf strong," he said, not without admiration. "Tony told you the truth, too – we got paid for this job before we started, and there's nobody to report to."

Jack regarded him silently, and then jerked his head.

"Out, you thug!" he said tersely, and the man went sideways into the fog, one eye glued to Jack Bryce's varnished boots.

That young man went back to his lodgings puzzled, and the next morning made a call upon Mr Hemmer, of Hemmer & Hemmer, the eminent solicitors, and gave an account of what had happened the previous night.

"I'm puzzled," he remarked. "I don't know any of our victims who bear ill-will, or have sufficient courage to tackle a job like this. Do you, sir?"

Mr Hemmer shook his head.

"No," he said. "If it had happened tomorrow or the next day I should have understood it, because I have a queer kind of job for you, and one which might very easily provoke some such outrage against your person as you experienced last night."

Jack looked at him with interest.

"Sit down," said Mr Hemmer, and when he had obeyed the lawyer leant his elbows on the table and lowered his voice. "I've always told you, Captain Bryce, that I would never give you a job which was outside the law, or which in any way brought you into conflict with the authorities. I am an officer of the Supreme Court, as all solicitors are ex-officio, and therefore it would not become me, and it would be grossly improper, if I suggested a line of conduct to you which in any way brought about a breach of the peace – do you know Joseph Sittingborn?" he asked suddenly.

"I know Sittingborn, the town," smiled Jack, "but not Joe of that ilk."

"I'm surprised," said the lawyer, a little disappointed. "I thought everybody knew Sittingborn. He is a big diamond merchant, in addition to which I believe he is a moneylender, and accommodates society people with short-term loans."

"That means that he has another name," laughed Jack, and Mr Hemmer looked embarrassed.

"Well, to be perfectly candid," he admitted hesitatingly, "his real name is Kultz, but I did not feel justified in mentioning that fact, because he is an old client of mine. I don't think, however, that I am betraying any confidence as between client and solicitor, because it is generally known in business circles that Sittingborn is an assumed name."

"I have an idea," said Jack, "that I shall be especially interested in your Sittingborn, Mr Hemmer, for I have a vague notion that this new case has something to do with the very unpleasant experience last night."

"It is not impossible that he had something to do with it, because the man is in touch with some of the greatest ruffians in London, and it was the information supplied to me by the police that he was connected with certain shady transactions which induced me to relinquish his work. But I don't see how – "

He scratched his chin with a puzzled air.

"Just one moment," he said, and went into an inner sanctum, where he kept his telephone, closing the door behind him.

In five minutes he returned.

"I'm afraid Lady Sybil Creen has been very indiscreet," he remarked.

"Lady Sybil Creen?" repeated Jack in surprise, for he knew the name of this society beauty, whose marriage to John Creen, the African millionaire, had been one of the sensations of the London season two years before.

"Lady Sybil met Sittingborn yesterday at the Carlton," said the lawyer, "and very foolishly told him that she was employing somebody to recover the Vlakfontain diamond."

Jack gasped.

"The Vlakfontain diamond?" he exclaimed, rising from his chair. "Good lord, has that been lost?"

"Sit down," said the lawyer. "I'll tell you. I'm very annoyed with Lady Sybil because, evidently, she put Sittingborn on to your track.

You're not without fame in the City of London, you know," he smiled, "and it is likely that Sittingborn put two and two together, with the result that he decided to jump in first and incapacitate you before you incapacitated him.

"Now, these are the facts," he went on. "Lady Sybil is a very bright, gay, young lady who is fond of her husband, but is also very fond of gambling. Her husband has forbidden her after her recent heavy losses to exceed a certain sum per annum, which, I need hardly say, is a very generous one. He had to go out to South Africa, leaving his wife behind, and during his absence Lady Sybil very unfortunately incurred heavy debts, losing tremendous sums at Deauville and Aix. As far as I can find out, Sittingborn is in love with Lady Sybil's sister, Lady Margaret, and as Lady Sybil, by reason of her marriage, dominates the impecunious household of her father, the Earl, there is no doubt that at a word from Lady Sybil, Sittingborn would be accepted.

"Well, as I say, the young lady lost a tremendous lot of money, and when she came back to London she found she had heavy bills to meet and no money to meet them with. She dare not cable to her husband, or see her husband's agents. Then it was that Sittingborn offered to lend her a very large sum indeed, providing she lodged as security the Vlakfontain diamond, which, as you know, is a very rare stone, and the gem of John Creen's collection.

"Lady Sybil foolishly agreed, for her half yearly allowance was due in a fortnight, and she knew she could redeem the stone. The transaction went through in the ordinary course. She placed the diamond, which was kept in her husband's safe, to which she had the key, in Sittingborn's possession, and received the money in exchange.

"At the end of a fortnight her money came in, and she went to Sittingborn to redeem the stone, and once that was in her possession she wrote to him, telling him that if he had held out any hope that her sister would marry him he must dismiss that possibility from his mind. I rather fancy Lady Sybil, in order to get the money, had very improperly encouraged such hopes in our friend. There the matter might have ended, and, as she thought, had ended; but that night Sittingborn was announced.

"She refused to see him at first, but the few words he wrote on a scrap of paper made her change her mind.

" 'So you thought you had got rid of me, did you, Lady Sybil?' he said, and then revealed his duplicity, for the stone he had handed back to the girl when she paid the money was merely a replica, a very clever copy in crystal, of the Vlakfontain diamond, which was still in his possession."

"But surely that's a criminal offence?"

"It is a criminal offence," said the lawyer; "but the one thing we do not want to happen, Lady Sybil and I, is that the fact should come out that she ever pledged the Vlakfontain diamond. Sittingborn would, of course, get seven years for fraud and conspiracy to defraud, but he knows very well that we are not going to take the case into Court, except as a last resort. Bryce, you've got to get that diamond from the man."

"By force?" asked Jack slowly.

"If necessary," said the lawyer, dropping his voice; "and I want to forget that I, a respectable officer of the court, ever suggested such a means, but we've got to get the diamond before Lady Sybil's husband returns from Africa in a month. Remember this, too," he added, "that Sittingborn is very much in the same predicament that we are. If we take the stone from him by violence he cannot make any trouble."

"Then it will be pretty easy," said Jack cheerfully, as he rose.

"Not so easy as you think," said Hemmer gravely. "You saw the other night what happened. The man has surrounded himself with a bodyguard, who will not hesitate to shoot. Remember, there's no excuse for you, either; and if you're shot dead in the attempt to take this stone by violence, he has a justification for his act. This game has got to be played on both sides just a little outside the law."

Jack stood in the centre of the room fingering his chin, his head bent downwards.

"Where does he keep this stone?" he asked.

"I have reason to believe that he carries it about with him," said the lawyer with the faintest of smiles. "Don't forget that he has three men, all of whom are heavily armed, within call, and two of these usually accompany him when he goes out. He is playing for big stakes, a society marriage the reward, and penal servitude the punishment."

"The more guards he has the better," remarked Jack cheerfully. "Nothing ruins a man so effectually as over-confidence."

He waited for a day before he made his call upon Mr Sittingborn's office in New Bond Street. He was conscious that during the time he had been closely watched. As a matter of fact, he had been shadowed carefully from the moment he left his house that morning to call upon Hemmer, and at night, looking through the blind, he saw a sleuth on duty on the other side of the road. If they expected any furtive plot, if they imagined he would go to the police or would make any elaborate preparations, Mr Sittingborn and his associates were mistaken.

At half-past three in the afternoon Jack stepped into the lift of the offices and was whisked up to the fourth floor, where Sittingborn had his suite. A man stepped into the lift with him, and Jack smiled inwardly, recognizing one of his shadows.

The precautions which Mr Sittingborn had taken were very clear to Jack as soon as he entered the outer office. Sittingborn's suite consisted of three rooms, in the first of which two clerks were working, and two men, who apparently were visitors waiting to transact business, were sitting comfortably reading newspapers.

They glanced up as soon as Jack entered, and both men rose.

Jack's plan was only half-formed, but such as it was it depended for its success upon whether or not Sittingborn indulged in the luxury of a private secretary. Such doubts as he had on this subject were set at rest after he had handed his card to one of the clerks.

The man looked at the name dubiously.

"Mr Sittingborn is engaged," he said. "Will you see Mr Jolly, his secretary?"

Jack nodded.

"One moment," said the clerk, and disappeared into the second room.

He came back after a long interval, and beckoned the visitor forward, and Jack noticed that the two men closed up behind him, although they did not enter the room, and stationed themselves near the door.

Mr Jolly proved to be ill-named, for he was a melancholy young man, with a very high collar and a lounge suit – Jack particularly noticed the lounge suit, because if the man had been wearing a morning coat his scheme would have come to naught.

"Good morning, Captain Bryce," said the pale Mr Jolly nervously. "What can I do for you?"

"I want to see Mr Sittingborn," Jack told him, with a side glance at the door marked "Private," which he knew must be Mr Sittingborn's offices.

There was no sound of voices, so the story of the diamond merchant being engaged was obviously fictitious.

"You can't see Mr Sittingborn," declared the secretary in a loud voice, and Jack realized that this was intended for the two men outside the door to hear.

"I must see Mr Sittingborn," said Jack calmly. "I have come with an offer from Lady Sybil. Will you tell him that Lady Sybil will agree to his terms with certain reservations."

There was no need to carry that message to the inner room, for somebody else had been listening, and the door to Mr Sittingborn's sanctum opened suddenly, and he appeared, a stockily built man, rather pasty of face, and with a slight, black moustache that served to emphasize the breadth of his countenance.

"Come in," he said. "You come in, too, Jolly. I've got no secrets from my secretary, and I'm certainly not going to see you alone, Bryce."

Jack chuckled, and followed Jolly into the office.

"Sit down there where I can see you," said Sittingborn, with a slight accent, and indicated a chair on the opposite side of his desk to where he now seated himself. "You sit over there, Jolly, where you can see this gentleman, too; and, in case you've any misapprehensions, Mr Bryce, as to what I'll do if you come any of your monkey tricks, just take a look at this."

Jack looked round carelessly at the open drawer on the further side of the desk, and saw an automatic pistol conspicuously displayed.

"Now, Mr Bryce, let's have your business. What have you come for?"

"I've come to get the Vlakfontain diamond," said Jack.

"Rubbish!" ejaculated the other. "I've got no Vlakfontain diamond! You can tell Hemmer – I suppose he sent you – that he ought to know that by now. He had my safe burgled two nights ago," he grinned; and Jack inwardly commended the lawyer upon his enterprise. "You can save yourself the trouble of searching my office," Sittingborn went on; "I know a much safer place," and he instinctively touched his breast pocket.

Jack had hoped to locate the diamond by other means. He knew that the man was carrying it about with him, but when only seconds were available it was vitally necessary to know in which pocket the stone was. And because of his confidence – that fatal confidence upon which Jack Bryce depended – Sittingborn had volunteered the information Jack desired.

The two men looked at one another. Mr Jolly, a nervous third, sat at the end of the desk alternately looking at both.

"Well, what's your offer?" asked Sittingborn.

One of his hands rested within a few inches of the pistol, and Jack was very anxious that that hand should come back. Again fortune favoured him. Sittingborn reached out, struck a match to light a cigar, using his left hand.

"Here is the offer," said Jack, and pulled a paper from his pocket, and instinctively the other hand came forward.

At that second Jack lifted the writing-table and flung it over. Half rising from his chair, Sittingborn staggered to his feet, his hand groping for the pistol now beyond his reach, and at that moment Jack caught him by the collar and hauled him across the wreckage.

The man was strong, but he was a child in the hands of Wireless Bryce. A second later Jack had dived into the pocket, had felt something hard wrapped up in cotton-wool, and had jerked it out, and then Jolly sprang at him with a shout, and there were sounds of feet in the outer office.

Jack turned to grapple with his assailant, and for a second they swayed, then Jolly fell with a crash against the partition. Then, as the door burst open, Jack raised his hand. Something flashing and brilliant hurtled through the air, smashed through the glass window, and disappeared into the busy street outside.

"There's your diamond," said Jack coolly. "Now, what are you going to do about it?"

He turned to confront the levelled muzzles of two pistols and grinned. Sittingborn was as white as death.

"You fool! You fool!" he cried hoarsely. "Do you know what you've done? You've thrown £200,000 into the street. What a complication!"

Then his eyes narrowed.

"Search him," he said, and under the pistol point Jack submitted to as thorough a search as he had ever experienced. They stripped his boots from his feet, and partially undressed him.

"There's nothing here," said one of the men, and Sittingborn groaned.

"I hoped the fool had thrown something else by mistake."

"What have I thrown?" asked Jack innocently.

"The Vlakfontain diamond, you scoundrel!" roared Sittingborn.

"But you said you hadn't got it," said Jack; and then, as he put on his coat, "you can send your thugs away, Kultz," he remarked, "and then you and I will have a little talk. This means imprisonment for you."

Mr Sittingborn was shaking.

"They can prove nothing," he said harshly; "nothing! Good lord! What a mess we're in!"

"Say 'I'm in,'" said Jack carefully. "Now, look here," he sat down, "you'd best come to Hemmer and straighten this matter out."

Just then Mr Jolly came in. He had been sent down into the street to look for the stone, but apparently his search had been unsuccessful.

"Not a sign of it," he reported. "It may have dropped on top of a motor bus."

"It's your fault," snarled Sittingborn, glaring at Jack, "and Hemmer's got to take the responsibility for employing a fool like you!"

"I'm going to explain that to Mr Hemmer, and I'm going to tell the truth about it," said Jack. "And either you or Jolly, or both, if you prefer, can come with me to confirm my statement."

"You bet I'm not going to let you get in the first story," said Sittingborn, struggling into his overcoat. "Now, Jolly, you saw what happened."

Half an hour later they sat in Mr Hemmer's musty office, and Jack told his story, and, to Sittingborn's surprise, the account he gave was an accurate one.

"There, you see," said Mr Sittingborn triumphantly, "this man admits he threw the thing into the street, and I am not responsible."

"It was the Vlakfontain diamond, then," said Hemmer gravely, and after a moment's hesitation the other nodded.

"You said you hadn't got it, you know, when I asked you," remarked Hemmer dryly.

"It was a joke," replied the dogged Mr Sittingborn.

"A pretty poor joke for you, Mr Sittingborn, if we had proceeded with this case. As it is, I'm rather bewildered," he said, turning to Jack.

Jack was sitting next to Mr Jolly, and suddenly he jerked that astonished young man to his feet by one arm. Jack plunged his disengaged hand into the pockets of the secretary, brought out something wrapped in cotton-wool, and laid it on Hemmer's table.

"There's the diamond, Mr Hemmer," he said; "I put it into Jolly's pocket for safety. Sittingborn said that he had infinite confidence in Jolly."

Sittingborn was on his feet, his mouth open.

"But – but – " he stammered, "when did you – "

"When I was grappling with him I put the diamond in his pocket," said Jack. "The stone I threw was the replica with which Mr Hemmer kindly provided me."

He opened the door, and made a gesture to Sittingborn.

"We've finished with you," he remarked pleasantly, "and when you marry Lady Margaret will you send me a piece of your wedding cake?"

A QUESTION OF HOURS

There are skeletons in a great many cupboards, and at some time the skeleton is of more terrifying proportions and appearance than is the case at others. The skeleton in Mrs Tewkesbury's cupboard appeared to her one of the more terrible variety, and she seldom opened the door for her own amusement.

Mr Hemmer, of the firm of Hemmer & Hemmer, solicitors, was, on the contrary, a connoisseur of family skeletons, and could examine them alone or in company without so much as flickering an eyelid.

Mrs Tewkesbury sat with Mr Hemmer one day in his private office, and slowly and haltingly sketched the outline of her own particular skeleton, and Mr Hemmer was unusually grave.

"Let me get the facts of the matter right, Mrs Tewkesbury," he said, consulting a pencilled slip before him. "When you married Mr Tewkesbury you were under the impression that you were a widow?"

The girl nodded. She was a slight, pretty woman, with a strained and frightened expression.

"You were married for the second time on the 15th of March, 1917, and later you discovered that your first husband was living long after you thought he was dead, and had, in fact, died on March 14, 1917, a day before you were married?"

"That is so," said the girl. "You see, Harold and I had parted. He was a wild sort of man, and never found any happiness in our life at home. He had spent many years in Western Australia, and three months after we were married he went out again, and I heard no more from him until I received a clipping from a newspaper saying that, whilst prospecting, he had died, and that he had died on the date I have given you."

Mr Hemmer nodded.

"So that if he did die on March 14, your marriage is legal. If, as this man Grimwald suggests, he died on March 16, you have, in fact, committed bigamy."

The lady inclined her head.

"Grimwald was with your husband when he died?"

Again the woman nodded.

"Yes, and I believe that is true, because in the Australian newspaper cutting his name was mentioned as having been with my husband; in fact, he brought the news to Onslow, which is a town in Western Australia."

"Now, just tell me this," proceeded Hemmer; "Grimwald demands money, but what does he promise, and what exactly does he say he will do unless you pay him?"

"He says the newspaper story was two days out, and he proves my husband did not die on the 14th – by the production of his diary, in which entries were made describing what had happened up to the night of the 15th, or rather up to the afternoon – my husband was killed by a fall of rock the next day after the last entry was made."

"Have you seen the diary?" asked Hemmer.

The lady nodded.

"There's no doubt it was written in Hal's hand," she said. "And what makes it beyond dispute as evidence is that he mentions an eclipse of the sun that occurred at sunset. I remember reading about it, and I have looked up the papers, and there is no question that the eclipse did occur that day."

"And the diary is in your husband's handwriting?"

"Yes."

Hemmer sat back in his chair.

"I am afraid, my dear lady," he said gently, "you are in rather a difficult position. If you are satisfied that that diary is in your husband's writing, and he was alive – as apparently he was – hours after you were married, you have committed bigamy."

She was silent.

"What does this man demand?"

"Nothing," said Mrs Tewkesbury bitterly.

"He does not put a price on his discretion, eh?" remarked Mr Hemmer thoughtfully. "That makes him a little dangerous, because it keeps him inside of the law. He simply states the facts and leaves the rest to you. Makes no promises, I suppose?"

She shook her head.

"I don't see how I can help you," said the lawyer, "particularly if you are satisfied that the man states the truth. After all, he is the only man who knew when your late husband died, and his word would be accepted, unless, of course, he stultified himself by playing the part of blackmailer, which, so far, he has not done. Now, I'll tell you what I will do, Mrs Tewkesbury," said Hemmer, ringing a bell. "I will send a man to you, and, if anybody can help you, he can. I want you to tell him all the facts just as you have told me."

A clerk came in.

"When could you see him?"

"I could see him at my hotel this afternoon," said the woman, and Hemmer nodded to the clerk.

"Call up Captain Bryce, and tell him to go to the Grand Imperial Hotel at – half-past three, shall we say?" The woman nodded. "To meet Mrs Tewkesbury."

"Who is Captain Bryce?" asked the girl curiously.

"Captain Bryce is a clever man," replied the other dryly. "I rather fancy you will like him."

Mr George Grimwald was a rugged specimen of humanity, with one of those faces which seemed different from every angle from whence it was viewed. He sat at the open window of his lodgings off the Gray's Inn Road, smoking a pipe of content. He was dressed airily in a pair of old khaki breeches, and a woollen shirt, the sleeves of which were rolled up to his elbows, exposing a brawny arm.

He descended from the window-sill as a knock came to the door.

"There's a gentleman wants to see you," said his landlady.

Mr George Grimwald stroked his scrubby moustache thoughtfully.

"Let him come up here," he said after a while.

He was not a man who was easily scared. At the moment, at any rate, he was conscious of his own rectitude, for he had not erred in the ways of vulgar blackmailers, and he might defy with some pride any person in the world, in which category he included Mrs Tewkesbury, to produce a scrap of paper which would lead to his undoing.

The visitor proved to be a tall, good-looking young man in a grey lounge suit, and Grimwald eyed him critically. He did not look like a detective; he was certainly unlike any lawyer the man had ever seen. Grimwald wrongly classified him as belonging to the idle rich – one of those young men about town who had nothing to do but to kill time and pheasants.

"Sit down, guv'nor. I don't know your name."

"My name is Bryce – Captain Jack Bryce," the visitor informed him. "You're Mr Grimwald, I presume?"

"That's me," said the other, "though you needn't trouble about mistering me, because I'm a very plain, matter-of-fact man, who doesn't stand on ceremony."

Jack selected one of the less rickety chairs and seated himself carefully.

"I'm a friend of Mrs Tewkesbury," he went on.

"Oh, you are, are you?" said the other with a little grin. "Well, any friend of Mrs Tewkesbury's a friend of mine. I knew a relation of hers very well, as I dare say she's told you."

"Her late husband," said Jack.

"A little bit too late," guffawed the other.

"About twenty-four hours, to be exact. Well, Cuthbert – we used to call him Cuthbert – wasn't a bad bloke as blokes went. He often used to say to me he'd make my fortune, but it hasn't come yet."

He turned his small, shrewd eyes in Jack's direction, and added slowly: "And when it does come, I'm not going to ask for it, you see."

"What is your idea of a fortune?" asked Jack carelessly.

"Oh, about ten thousand pounds," said the other indifferently. "It's likely to happen, you know. Perhaps one of these days some young lady will take a fancy to me and hand me over ten thousand of the brightest and best."

"On condition that you keep your mouth shut, eh?" remarked Jack.

"What d'yer mean?" demanded the other indignantly. "I didn't say anything about keeping my mouth shut, did I? I haven't asked for money from anybody, have I? I don't understand you, mister."

"You understand me all right," said Jack easily. "You've come over here to blackmail Mrs Tewkesbury. You've come with a cock-and-bull story about her husband having died after her second marriage, and you want ten thousand pounds to keep your mouth shut."

The man gaped at him, and an angry red crept into his face.

"Look here, young shaver," he said, "you keep a civil tongue in your head, or d'yer know what I'll do to you?"

"Tell me," said Jack.

"I'll take you by the scruff of your neck and chuck you out of that window. What are you laughing at?"

Jack was laughing silently.

"I don't think you will," he remarked softly. "Now, let's be sensible, Mr – or Grimwald, if you will pardon the familiarity."

He picked up a piece of wood which was employed by the landlady to keep the window from closing, for the sash lines were out of order.

"I want you to take my point of view in this matter," he went on, "and to realize that violence of any kind is repugnant to me."

As he spoke he snapped off a piece of wood an inch from the end of the stick, and Grimwald stared at him.

"Violence I loathe," pursued Jack. "It rumples your shirt and increases your laundry bill."

Snap went another piece of wood. "And, what's more," snap went a third piece of wood.

"Here, let's have a look at that bit of wood, guv'nor," said Grimwald, his curiosity getting the better of him. "It must be pretty rotten for you to be able to snap it off with your fingers like that."

Jack handed over the wood, and the man tried, but failed even to bend the stick, though he strained in an effort to emulate the feat of his visitor.

He put the wood down, and looked at Jack with a new respect. Then, reaching out gingerly, he gripped the visitor's arm, and his big hand closed round Wireless Bryce's biceps. He let go and whistled.

"I told you I'd throw you out of the window, didn't I?" he said.

"I think you mentioned something of the sort."

"Well, that arrangement's off," declared Grimwald, and laughed.

Jack laughed, too.

"Now I think we're beginning to understand one another. And I want you to proceed with your grand little scheme, Grimwald."

"There ain't any scheme," said Grimwald, thrusting his hands in his trousers pockets. "I simply know a few facts, and I've made them known in the proper quarter. I asked for no money, because that would be blackmail, and blackmail is repugnant to my feelings. I was well brought up, and sang in the choir when I was younger."

"Most of the prisons have choirs," said Jack calmly. "Don't let us talk about your unpleasant past. Now, what are we going to do about Mrs Tewkesbury? Suppose I offer you a thousand pounds?"

A slow smile dawned on the other's face. "A thousand pounds!" he scoffed. "Why, you're trying to bribe me to commit blackmail. And as I've told you – "

"I know what you've told me," said Jack. "But I wasn't going to bribe you to commit blackmail, but to do something even more repugnant to your nature."

"What's that?" asked the other in some astonishment, as though the idea of there being anything too repugnant came as news to him.

"I want you to tell the truth," said Jack.

"But I've told it, haven't I? Cuthbert died on the 16th. The account of his having died on the 14th was the reporter's mix-up. I've shown Mrs Tewkesbury the diary, and she knows it's true. She's got a copy of it; I suppose she showed you?"

"Yes," nodded Jack. "I've got it here." He took a sheet of paper from his pocket. "Here is the extract." He opened the paper and read:

"March 14. – Decided to stay here for a couple of days."

"That's the only entry on that date."
"That's right," nodded the other.

"March 15," read Jack. "Grimm found some old caves, and said that there was a sign of ancient workings. Went with him and explored same. Took samples of rock. Washed same; they showed colour."

"That means they showed gold," said Grimwald.

"Towards sunset we saw wonderful eclipse of the sun. Very awe-inspiring."

He refolded the paper.
"That's the last entry," he commented.
"He was killed the next morning," explained Grimwald. "He was sleeping at the foot of a hill and there was a bit of a landslide, and a big rock boulder came down and smashed him up. Half-past six in the morning – eighteen hours after Mrs Tewkesbury was married."
"Where did you sleep that night?" Jack demanded suddenly, and the man looked at him, startled.
"Where did I sleep?" he repeated. "Why, I – I slept by the camp fire."
Jack had taken a newspaper cutting from his pocket, and was examining it.
"You told the reporter that after the accident you shifted your camp to the other side of the hill, and early in the morning you trekked for the town of Onslow."
"Well, what about it?" Grimwald asked defiantly. "There's nothing in that, is there?"
"Listen to this," said Jack, and read – " 'I shifted my camp to the other side of the hill to avoid any falling boulders, and then, as soon

as it was light I started off to walk into the nearest town, bringing my partner's papers.'

"Including," said Jack, looking up, "the letters which Mrs Tewkesbury had written to her husband, and which he had not answered. And from those letters you discovered her address, and, finding she was married, you concocted this little scheme to make your fortune."

The man's eyes glinted dangerously.

"That's a lie," he growled. "But, anyway, what does that paper prove?"

"It proves that the accident occurred on the previous day," said Jack. "And that is why I'm offering you the sum of one thousand pounds for the truth, whether it favours Mrs Tewkesbury or whether it does not favour her. And," he added significantly, "this sum is distinct from any sum you may further receive should the lady in a generous mood wish to pay you for your other services."

The man was silent for a long time.

"Well, I don't know that it makes much difference," he said, "hours or days. Now I'll tell the truth, guv'nor, and I'm prepared to swear to it before a lawyer, though I'm not going to incriminate myself by saying I want money for keeping my mouth shut or anything like that."

"I shan't ask you to commit yourself to that extent," Jack told him with a faint smile. "Now, Grimwald, let's have the truth."

"You shall have it," grinned the man, "and much good may it do Mrs Tewkesbury. This is the story: "We were camped by the side of the hill, as I have said, but we were not alone. We had an Australian native with us, a chap called Tikilivi, who can be found to prove my words, because he's a missionary boy and can talk English. It was just after the sun went down, whilst I was sitting by the fire making some damper, that Cuthbert said he guessed he would lie down for an hour, as he was feeling tired. He had hardly rolled himself in his blanket before that dashed landslide began, and he was dead before I could reach him. A big boulder had rolled right down on him, and was resting on him. It took me and the boy about an hour to get it off him."

"What time was this?" asked Jack.

"Six o'clock. There was still light in the sky, and Tikilivi will swear to it."

Jack rose.

"If you're prepared to put that statement into an affidavit, I'm prepared to give you the thousand pounds."

He accompanied the man to the office of Hemmer & Hemmer. Mr Hemmer was out, but his managing clerk drew up the statement, which was sworn to before a neighbouring commissioner of oaths. Then Jack handed him a cheque for a thousand pounds drawn by Mrs Tewkesbury.

Later he showed the statement to Hemmer, and the lawyer pulled a long face.

"I don't know how this helps us," he said. "In fact, it makes the matter a little worse than before. We knew, and Mrs Tewkesbury knew, that the man's statement was practically true, and that she had, in fact, committed bigamy. What are you going to do now?"

Jack chuckled.

"I'm going to wait for Mr Grimwald to make his next move."

He had not long to wait. Three days later an urgent telephone call took him to Mrs Tewkesbury.

"I've seen Grimwald," she said, obviously distressed.

"Well?" asked Jack. "What is he going to do?"

The lady paced the apartment, beside herself with apprehension.

"He told me that he knew I had married a very rich man, and that Mr Tewkesbury had settled a large sum of money upon me," she said.

"That didn't want much finding out," smiled Jack. "What else?"

"He said that he was going to tell the whole story of Harold's death to the newspapers. What am I to do, Captain Bryce? We know now the very worst. Do you think he is likely to carry out his threat?"

Jack nodded.

"I think it is very likely. He's a rough and uncouth person, but he seems to have the gift of narrative, and in the cutting from the Australian paper which you gave me, you will remember that it spoke of him as the man who gave such an interesting account of his trek across the great desert. Moreover," he said, "I can give you this information, that he has engaged a stenographer, and he's now busy upon the production of his story. He would do this naturally," he went on, "because it would relieve him from any suggestion of blackmail; or, at any rate, if the story is in existence, there would be a greater difficulty in proving that his whole object in telling the story was to induce you to buy it for ten thousand pounds. Does your husband know?"

She nodded.

"I told him everything. Would you like to see him?"

She put her hand to the bell, but Jack checked her with a gesture.

"I don't think so," he said. "But you might tell him from me that neither he nor you need be in any way alarmed. I will guarantee that that story is never published."

She looked at him in astonishment.

"Do you really mean that?" she demanded eagerly.

He nodded.

"I am now going round to see Mr Grimwald," he said, picking up his hat, "and possibly I may assist him in his literary pursuits. I've a little gift that way myself."

He found Mr Grimwald wrestling in the agonies of composition. A girl from a typewriting agency sat at one side of the table, Mr Grimwald, in his shirtsleeves, sat at the other, and he looked up with a malicious little smile as Jack came in.

"Hullo! Busy, Grimwald?" asked the visitor with well-affected carelessness.

"Just writing a bit of a story, old man," said Grimwald. "Sit down. It will interest you to hear it."

"I didn't know you were a literary gent," said Jack, pulling up a chair.

"Literature is an easy thing to me," declared Grimwald. "Now, miss, you got to the part where I said that Mrs Tewkesbury was married to her husband in St George's Church at half-past two on the 14th March."

All this was intended for Jack, as he well knew.

"Now, miss," said the biographer, "I'll now proceed to tell how her husband – her rightful husband, you understand – was killed at half-past six on the same day."

"At half-past ten," murmured Jack.

The man swung round on him.

"Half-past six," he said slowly, "and I can prove it."

"Half-past ten," repeated Jack. "Four hours before Mrs Tewkesbury was married."

"You're mad!" laughed the other. "I can prove it again and again. Half-past ten!" he sneered, "when the eclipse didn't occur till sunset, and Mrs Tewkesbury admits it was her husband's handwriting. Do you doubt that?"

"I admit that the entry in the diary was in his handwriting. I admit that he saw an eclipse at sunset," said Jack gently. "Nevertheless, he died at half-past ten in the morning."

"Have you gone off your head?" asked the other.

Jack shook his head.

"My poor Grimwald," he said, "there is eight hours difference in the time between Western Australia and London. Half-past six in Western Australia is half-past ten in Great Britain. So Mrs Tewkesbury was married four hours after her husband's death."

The man stared at him; then, with a curse, pushed back his chair, and stood up from the table. He nodded to the girl, who was watching him.

"That'll do, miss," he said. "I shan't want you again."

When she had gone out, he turned to Jack.

"I ought to have stuck to the next-morning story," he said. "I thought I was safe when I told the truth."

"Very few of us would be safe if we told the truth," remarked Jack sententiously. "And, anyway, you have had a thousand pounds for telling it, Grimwald."

A slow smile lit Grimwald's rugged face.

"That's something," he said with satisfaction. "Do you know what I'd like to do if I didn't know you? I'd like to fight you for that thousand pounds."

Jack looked at him steadily.

"You can, if you like," he said. But Mr Grimwald, remembering the size of the biceps under that well-tailored jacket – remembering, too, the piece of stout wood that Jack had broken as though it were made of pith – decided that, on the whole, he wouldn't.

THE STRANGE CASE OF ANITA BRADE

No man realized more thoroughly the extent of the good fortune which had come his way, or recognized more fairly the element of luck which had contributed to his success, than Jack Bryce. In the space of a few months he had built up for himself, out of nothing more tangible than opportunity, a record which not only benefited him and added weekly to the respectable sum which he had standing to his credit at the bank, but had added something to the prestige of his employer.

Between Mr Hemmer and his assistant something like a close, personal friendship had sprung up. That this state of affairs was to Jack Bryce's advantage need not be questioned. But to some extent it also embarrassed him.

In the early days the solicitor had given him cases which might be described as forlorn hopes, and Jack had succeeded beyond all expectations. Now, however, Mr Hemmer was growing more cautious.

"I can't afford that you should have a failure, Bryce," he said one morning. "I want your record to be one of continuous success."

"I have a preference for that also," said Jack with twitching lips, "but it will never do for you to give me only the soft jobs."

"Why not?"

"Because," the other answered, "there's no better way of dulling the edge of the keenest blade than putting it to cut paper."

They were breakfasting together at Mr Hemmer's house in Savile Square, and the lawyer smiled grimly as he folded his serviette and laid it on the table.

"I won't give you easy jobs," he said; "but I don't want to give you fiddling jobs. For example, I should like to send you along to meet Anita Brade, but my managing clerk can do that." He paused. "Still, I would like somebody to see her who understands human nature as well as you do. The girl rather puzzles me."

"She rather interests me," said Jack with a smile. "Won't you tell me all about her?"

"With pleasure," said the lawyer. "Only I don't think there's a job in it for you, by which I mean I don't want anybody tossed over your head or half-strangled."

Jack laughed.

"Come down to the office with me," said the lawyer after a moment's thought, "and I'll tell you all about the matter on my way."

When they were in the big limousine Mr Hemmer explained something of his doubts.

"Anita Brade is the daughter of an old client of mine," he said, "Felix Brade, belonging to the North of England. He died about six years ago, when the girl was at school, leaving her about thirty thousand pounds, which she inherits on her twenty-first birthday – that is, in six months' time. Mrs Brade was a weak, amiable creature, and poor Felix had not been dead a few months before she met and was married by a man for whom I have the most intense dislike – Mr Tallot Sordley. Sordley is one of those mysterious individuals who always keep up a good appearance and yet never seem to have any settled income or means of livelihood. Undoubtedly he was attractive, in a flashy sort of way, and the susceptible Mrs Brade fell a victim to his addresses. I don't know whether Sordley expected the woman to have money, but if he did he was disappointed. She had a very generous income, which ceased at her death, and this sad event took place about two years ago. Even the big house at Wittesden Park, where she lived and died, was the property of her daughter, and I rather fancy the discovery that her income ceased at her death came as a shock to Mr Sordley. I saw him once after the poor lady's decease, and he was a very indignant and agitated man.

"Unhappily for all concerned, Mrs Brade – or Mrs Sordley, as she became – transferred the guardianship of her daughter, Anita, to her husband. But I had, and retained, certain rights of access to the child, and every six months I pay her a visit, whilst every month she writes to me. It is also my duty to send her five hundred pounds a year, part of the interest which her legacy earns, and this I do every quarter.

"Now you may expect," he continued, turning with a quizzical smile to the other, "some sinister ending to this story. But, really, there is none. The girl seems perfectly happy, and her letters do not suggest otherwise. I have seen her once or twice, and my managing clerk has seen her once, and though she is a mysterious little creature, she gives a satisfying account of her life, and apparently both Tallot Sordley and his new wife – for he has married again – treat her very well."

"Not a very promising case from my point of view," observed Jack.

"No, it isn't," admitted the other. "But still – there are possibilities even in the most commonplace cases, as I have learnt as a lawyer."

When they reached the office he produced a bundle of letters and threw them across the table to Jack, and Bryce read them carefully.

"Nicely written, but very colourless," was his comment.

"Exactly," said the other. "They might have been copied from one of these books which profess to teach you the art of polite letter writing. Would you like to go down and see her? Today is the visiting day."

"I'd like to know," mused Jack, "if for no other reason, why she uses the word 'development' in every one of her letters."

"I didn't notice that," remarked the lawyer, raising his eyebrows. "But, anyway, it's a very commonplace word."

"Nevertheless, it's curious," said Jack.

That afternoon at three o'clock he found himself at Wittesden Park, which is a broad thoroughfare between Camberwell and Dulwich, made up of large houses, each detached from the other and standing in their own grounds. No. 79 Wittesden Park was a corner house, somewhat in need of repair, for the discoloured plaster with which it was covered had broken away in places and showed the naked brick beneath. The garden, too, was untidily kept; the grass was knee-high, and apparently no gardener was employed. But the appearance of the house was clean and bright; the curtains were white and the windows spotless.

Jack made a point of making a very complete survey of new grounds, and noted that there was a basement well beneath the level of the ground, and that the windows were barred, as the windows of such places are, and instead of curtains the panes were covered with blue wash, which he thought was unusual.

The door was opened to his knock by a sturdily built man of forty, with heavy, bushy eyebrows, which met above his aquiline nose, and a cheek and chin which suggested that their owner had not shaved that morning.

He greeted Jack with a broad smile of welcome – which seemed a bit surprising to Jack.

"You're from Mr Hemmer, I suppose?" he remarked politely. "Won't you step in?"

He shut the door behind Jack, and led the way to the front drawing-room, which was separated from another apartment by varnished folding doors.

"I will tell Anita," he said, and went out, leaving Jack to take stock of the room.

The folding doors apparently led to another room, in which Mr Hemmer's client was awaiting him, for he heard voices, and presently the door from the passage opened, and a girl came in. She was white of face, and her delicate features were rather pinched. She was well dressed in black alpaca, which must have been chosen for her when she was less painfully thin than she was at that moment, for there were places where it hung upon her like a sack.

"This is the gentleman from Mr Hemmer," introduced Tallot Sordley in a low, caressing voice.

Jack took the girl's hand in his, and experienced a shock. He recovered himself immediately before the keen-eyed Mr Sordley could notice the effect of that handshake, and said: "Mr Hemmer has sent me down to see you, Miss Brade. Is there anything you want?"

"Nothing," said the girl quietly.

"Are you – " Jack was at some loss as to how to proceed.

"I am perfectly happy, and having quite a good time," she remarked with a monotonous regularity of intonation which told the visitor a great deal.

He tried to make conversation, and found it difficult, and was a little relieved when an interview, which to him was acutely painful, ended by her rising and gliding from the room.

"My daughter is rather shy," remarked Mr Sordley. "Of course," he added, "I think her mental development isn't all it might be. But then, you know, girls change so quickly, and at any time we might see a development for the better."

"Oh, yes?" replied Jack politely, and made a little more conversation.

Presently he heard the word again; in fact, in the course of a quarter of an hour's conversation, Mr Sordley employed the word "development" seven times in seven different senses. It was a favourite word of his, and evidently all those grateful and pleasant letters which Miss Anita Brade had written had been dictated by this man, who could no more exclude the use of his favourite word than Mr Dick could exclude reference to King Charles' head.

Now all the time they were talking Jack was looking round. He was looking round still when they were in the hall, Mr Sordley obviously anxious to be rid of the visitor; and here his inspection was rewarded. On the first landing he saw, as he glanced up the stairs, that there was a small window of coloured glass, designed to give light to the stairway. He looked past Mr Sordley along the passage, and saw the door of a room – which was evidently either a breakfast-room or Mr Sordley's study. It proved to be the latter. From the roof of that study, he mentally noted, one must be able to reach that window.

Presently he took leave of his host, and walked down the six stone steps that led to the ill-kept garden, hearing the door slam behind him. Once outside the house he made a further survey, and found that his surmise was correct, and that there was a flat-roofed building, evidently erected after the house had been completed, and from that roof the coloured window was easily reached.

He made yet another reconnaissance, and then went home in a thoughtful mood. He got his employer on the telephone and expressed his suspicions.

"I'm going a little farther than you could wish in this matter," said Jack; "but I rather think I shall be justified."

"Go as far as you like," answered the lawyer; "but don't tell anybody I gave you authority."

That night the weather broke. A heavy gale came roaring up from the south-west, and rain fell incessantly. It was a night very suitable for Jack's purpose. Nine o'clock found him in the not too well-lighted thoroughfare of Wittesden Park, carrying a small black satchel slung over one shoulder.

He waited an opportunity, and then climbed the wall which separated the road from the back garden of Mr Sordley's house. The place was in darkness, but he guessed that all the shutters were closed – he had noticed folding shutters to the windows during his visit in the afternoon. He walked carefully through the garden, and came at last to the wall of the room which he had decided must be Sordley's study.

There were three big windows looking out upon the garden, and these were in darkness. He flashed a light from his electric lamp upon them, and found that they, too, were shuttered. He listened intently, but could hear nothing, and then he looked around for some means to reach the roof of the room.

Inside the house a different atmosphere prevailed from that which had marked the afternoon. In the underground kitchen were three people. Mr Sordley was the dominating figure. He was in his shirtsleeves, and there was no smile upon his heavy face. With him was a brassy-haired woman whose face was heavily rouged, and who wore a silk dress of expensive cut. Across her bosom was a diamond brooch which glittered and flashed in the light afforded by one miserable gas-burner. Jack might not have recognized in the girl who cringed before the couple the well-dressed, ethereal creature he had seen that afternoon. Her attitude was one of wilting terror, and her face was grimy. She wore a cotton dress, soiled and in holes, so that her sharp elbows were thrust into view, and on her feet, which were encased in nondescript slippers, was an odd pair of stockings.

She had reason to cringe, for the man assumed a very threatening attitude.

"And if I have any more of your nonsense, I'll knock your head off," the man was saying.

"You ought to be thankful you're alive," exclaimed the woman in a coarse voice. "I think Mr Sordley's too kind to you."

The girl said nothing.

"If your ma hadn't deceived Mr Sordley, and left all her money to you, things might have been different," the woman went on. "But she was a wicked, deceitful person."

"Don't talk about my mother," said the girl, firing up; and again the man threatened to strike the girl.

"Now, understand once and for all, Nita," said Sordley, "that there's no money for dresses for you. It takes all I can get from that lawyer to keep this house going. And you're going to stay here until your twenty-first birthday, and then you're going to draw the money that's due to you, and perhaps I'll let you have a bit of it."

"I can't do the work of the house," said the girl sullenly. "It's killing me. Couldn't you have a servant?"

"And have my business all over the neighbourhood! That'd be a pretty development," sneered Sordley.

"I want fresh air — I want to get out — I'm dying in this prison," said the girl, stung to madness by the hopelessness of her position.

"I dare say you do," replied Mr Sordley. He walked across the kitchen, and threw open the heavy door.

"You can go to bed now," he commanded, and the girl shivered.

"Couldn't I sleep upstairs?" she pleaded. "You've no idea how horrible it is there, with no light. And one can hear the mice."

"Get in," said Mr Sordley.

The girl lit a candle and went to the door of the room. The cold struck her like a whip, for this was a cellar — a wine cellar it had been in her father's days — and beyond a truckle bed and a chair there was no furniture.

"Oh, God, I wish I was dead!" she sobbed. "Oh, daddie, daddie, why did you leave me?"

"Well, he's left you all right," guffawed Mr Sordley. "And there's nobody going to worry their head about you."

"That's where you've made a mistake," said a voice behind him.

He turned in a flash. A man stood in the doorway, leisurely removing his raincoat. He had put a small black satchel at his feet, a bag containing a few implements which burglars employ in making their unauthorized entrances.

Sordley's face had gone a dirty white.

"What do you want?" he gasped, for he had recognized the visitor of the afternoon.

Jack did not reply. He turned his eyes to the girl standing open-mouthed at the door of her little cell − for cell it was, and no better − and with a jerk of his chin he beckoned her. She was halfway across the room when, with a howl like a beast, Sordley flung himself upon the intruder.

He did not attain his objective. A hand like the business end of a battering-ram caught him under the jaw, and he fell sprawling on the floor. The woman was not so easy to manage, when, with a scream, she flew at Jack like a tiger. But he caught her in his arms, and, pinioning her elbows to her side, shook her as certain mothers shake their naughty children.

"Come here, my dear," said Jack kindly, and the girl came shrinking towards him. "Go upstairs and make yourself presentable. Have a little wine, if there is any in the house. And choose for yourself the best bedroom."

Sordley was climbing up to his feet as the girl flitted from the kitchen.

"You'll pay for this," he growled. "I'll have the police to you."

"Not yet," said Jack softly.

He stooped and picked up a whip which the man had dropped.

"I thought I heard that being used," he said. "Take your coat off, Sordley."

"What do you mean?"

"Do as you are told. Take your coat off." He looked round. There was a heap of dishes in the kitchen sink, evidently left over from the day. He found later that it was the girl's duty to wash them up in the morning, and that she had to get up at five o'clock for the purpose.

"Wash those plates," said Jack. "You can wash and your wife can wipe."

The man snarled forth a blasphemous refusal.

And then the lash of the whip stung across his face. Again the woman sprung up with a whimper of rage.

"Keep your distance, my good friend," said Jack. "I can't hurt you, but I'll give your husband two – one for him and one for you. Wash those plates."

Without a word they obeyed. Jack, sitting on the kitchen table, a pipe clenched between his teeth, watched the operation with quiet interest.

"Now," he said, "you can go to bed." They made for the door that led to the stairs, but Jack put himself before it.

"When I said 'to bed,' " he said, "I mean to the bed which you assigned to Miss Brade." He pointed to the cellar entrance.

"But I can't sleep there!" gasped the man. "There isn't room for two."

"Make room," said Jack.

"I'll see you – " began the man. But the whip came up again, and he leapt back with a cry of alarm.

"You'll pay for this," said the woman, shaking with temper. "How am I to sleep there without my night things?"

"How was Miss Brade to sleep there?" asked Jack sternly. "Get in. You're too talkative, both of you."

The whip cracked at Sordley's heels, and he jumped again. Jack pulled to the door of their sleeping-room and locked it. Then he went upstairs and found the girl sitting in the drawing-room in a condition bordering upon collapse.

Falteringly, incoherently, she told her story. On her mother's death Sordley had brought his new wife home, and then had begun a period of slavery for her, unrelieved by any moment of happiness.

"I wrote to Mr Hemmer at their dictation," she said.

"I know that," nodded Jack; "and I suppose you were carefully coached in what you had to say when Mr Hemmer's visitor called? Now, my dear," he said, "you've got to stay here tonight, but to-morrow morning you shall go up and see Mr Hemmer, and he will arrange for your future."

"But what of Mr Sordley?" she asked.

"He's all right," said Jack. "I'll go down and see him in the morning. By the way," he asked as the girl was leaving the room, "what does Mr Sordley do for a living besides take your allowance?"

She shook her head.

"I don't know," she confessed. "Mr Sordley has a lot of friends – men mostly – who come here, generally at night. I think he has some sort of business which is not quite – " She hesitated.

"Quite legal, eh?"

"That's what I think," she said. "I heard him once saying that when my money came to him, he wouldn't take any more risks; and once, in the last month of the war, after a policeman called at the house because too much light was showing from the fanlight, Mr Sordley had some sort of fit."

Jack whistled.

"Oh, it's like that, is it?" he said. "Well, that makes things easy."

The next morning at six o'clock he was in the kitchen. He had slept that night on the sofa in the drawing-room, partly because it was over the place where the prisoners were confined, and partly because he wanted to be at hand in case anything developed (he smiled as he thought the word) during the night.

He unlocked the door of the prison house, and Sordley came out, blinking, into the light.

"Make some tea for me, with buttered toast," ordered Jack, "and be sharp about it."

He carried in his hand the whip which he regarded as his wand of office, and, without a word, Sordley began to kindle the fire. He was joined in a few minutes by his wife, looking a little bedraggled and old in the early hours of the morning.

"You, madam," continued Jack, "can go upstairs and tidy the drawing-room. Afterwards, when Miss Brade has left, you can make the bed, and generally put the house in order."

"When Miss Brade has left! Where's she going?" asked Sordley, turning round from his task.

Jack swung towards Sordley in what seemed to be a rather vicious manner.

"When I want you to talk, I'll tell you," he said.

"What are you going to do with us?" asked the woman.

"You're going to have a week of the life which you led that unfortunate girl," said Jack deliberately. "You're going to do the work I appoint, and you're going to get severe trouble if you don't, both of you."

Jack went upstairs and began to explore the house. On the top floor he found a room, the door of which defied his efforts to open. He went down and saw the girl.

"That's Mr Sordley's own room," said Anita. "I have never been inside it, and I don't think anybody else has."

"Is there a key?"

She shook her head.

"Mr Sordley carries that," she said. "He'll give it to you, won't he?"

Jack smiled.

"I think he would, if I wanted it," he said, "but at the moment I will save him the trouble."

He went back to the landing whence the room opened, and presently the girl heard a crash of breaking wood, and ran upstairs in alarm. The door was open, and Jack was viewing its interior with interest.

A great bench ran one length of the room, and on the bench were four beautiful little printing presses. Jack examined a plate which was still on the press, and laughed softly.

"I didn't know Mr Sordley was a printer," said Anita in wonder.

"A good many other people don't know it," replied Jack. "And quite a number will be interested to learn how Mr Sordley spent his spare time.

"Anyway," he said as he ushered the girl from the room, "this will save me a lot of trouble, for I did not look forward to a week's stay in this house."

He understood now why the place was run without prying servants, and why the girl had been kept like a bond-slave within its four walls.

When she came down dressed for her journey, carrying her pitiably few belongings in a little attaché case, she found him waiting in the hall, the door wide open.

"Here is a note," he said, handing her an envelope. "I should be glad if you would give this to the superintendent, or to the inspector, in charge of the nearest police station."

"Police station?" she faltered. "Are you going to – "

"Now, don't ask me questions," he said good-humouredly. "Just do as I tell you. I shall probably see you at Mr Hemmer's office in the course of the day."

He watched her out, closed the door, and walked, whistling, down into the kitchen, holding his whip by the lash, and swinging the butt in a circle. He arrived in time to see the two people engaged in an earnest conversation. They turned at the sound of Jack's footsteps, and Sordley came towards him.

"Look here, Mr What's-your-name," he proffered; "I've got a proposal to make to you. We'll allow Anita to leave the house – "

"You can save yourself the trouble; she's left," responded Jack.

"Well, we'll refund all the money we've had from her," said the man desperately, "on condition you leave the house."

"I intend leaving it today," replied Jack, and a look of relief came into the man's face.

A quarter of an hour later he was feeling very cheerful when Jack returned to the kitchen accompanied by two broad-shouldered men, one of whom slipped a pair of handcuffs on Sordley's wrist.

"What's the charge?" the man asked.

"Counterfeiting," said the detective cheerfully. "I've seen your printing press and some of the half-finished one-pound notes you've been making. You've got quite a plant upstairs, old man."

Sordley's knees gave way, and he would have fallen had not the detective gripped him by the arm. He turned a look of malignant hate upon Jack as the other detective gripped the arm of Mrs Sordley.

"One of these days," he snarled between his teeth, "I'll settle with you, my friend."

"You'll have to wait seven long years," replied Jack cheerfully.

"Ten," said the detective in sepulchral tones; "and he'll be lucky if he doesn't get a lifer."

THE DISAPPEARING LADY

"Jack," said Hemmer one morning when Captain Bryce had made his usual call upon his chief, "do you remember our friend Sittingborn?"

"The diamond merchant?" asked Jack with a little grin. "Yes; I remember him very well, sir."

"Humph!" grunted Mr Hemmer. "You wouldn't think he was an admirer of yours?"

Jack laughed. He had once spoiled a very pretty plan of Mr Kultz, alias Sittingborn, a plan which, had it succeeded, would have brought that gentleman into the exclusive ranks of British society, for he contemplated marrying the daughter of an aristocrat, and had virtually blackmailed the sister of the girl in the furtherance of his scheme.

"No," he said; "I shouldn't believe that, even if he told me."

"Well, apparently he is. I remarked to you some time ago that he was an old client of mine, and you may imagine my surprise, after what has occurred, when he came into my office yesterday afternoon in the most genial manner and asked me to let bygones be bygones."

"How touching!" said Jack, and the other smiled.

"Yes, it was a little staggering," he admitted; "but it takes a lot to stagger me. Anyway, to cut a long story short, we had a talk, in the course of which he said he harboured no malice towards you, and hoped that he'd be able to put some work in your way."

Jack was silent. He had too large a knowledge of the world to believe that a man of Sittingborn's temperament and mental calibre could forget or forgive. And his scepticism showed in his face.

"Is there to be an official reconciliation?" he asked ironically, and Mr Hemmer, that dry man of law, laughed.

"As a matter of fact, you're invited to Grosvenor Place to dine with him and his sister tonight."

"Oh, yes, and I'm to be murdered on the mat to make a Kultz's holiday?"

"You can please yourself about accepting, but there you are. No. 109 Grosvenor Place, and the hour is 7.30 for 8. It will be a little family dinner, with nobody else present but Mr Sittingborn and his charming sister Rebecca."

"I don't like her name," said Jack, "but I'll accept the invitation."

Accordingly he presented himself – and a fine figure of a man he looked in evening dress – at the hour of half-past seven, and a respectable, white-haired butler ushered him into the drawing-room.

Mr Sittingborn came forward with both hands extended as though he were greeting the dearest friend his life had known.

"My good chap, how splendid of you to come! You know my sister? Perhaps you don't."

"I don't," admitted Jack.

The lady who bowed to him with the friendliest of smiles was an olive-faced girl, distinctly pretty, with large, slumberous eyes, and a perfect, oval face.

"My brother's been telling me about you. You are a wicked man," she laughed.

"Oh, clever, dashed clever!" said Mr Sittingborn, with a heartiness that would have deceived any less experienced man than Captain Jack Bryce. "Still, I don't bear him any malice. And, really, there are one or two jobs I want you to tackle for me, Bryce, if you don't mind."

Over dinner he confided what these jobs might be. There was a Madame Vashti, a Greek lady of considerable wealth, but eccentric, explained Mr Sittingborn. Jack had made himself acquainted with particulars about most of the wealthy and society people in London – that had been his one study in the past few months: and he had heard of Madame Vashti and her amazing collection of rubies.

"Madame and I have been quite good friends," explained Sittingborn; "but for some reason lately she has taken a violent dislike to my sister. I don't pretend to understand it, except that Madame Vashti is still young, and there is a gentleman who is rather attentive to Rebecca whom I know Madame Vashti is very keen about. You won't mind me telling you these family secrets?"

"I rather like them," said Jack silkily, and glanced at the girl, who seemed in no wise perturbed by these revelations of rivalry.

He was curious to discover just what Mr Sittingborn wanted of him. He was to learn without delay, for the next sentence told him just what services would be required.

"I have good reason to know," remarked Mr Sittingborn, toying with his wine glass and smiling under his black moustache, "that you are something of a handy man with your fists, and that you're altogether reliable and suitable for the part I want you to play."

Jack said nothing, waiting to hear.

"The truth is," continued Mr Sittingborn in a burst of candour, "that I am not quite satisfied that my sister is safe."

"Safe?" repeated Jack in surprise, and Sittingborn nodded.

"Madame Vashti is a foreigner, and, I think, a very revengeful woman. I have had hints which I cannot afford to ignore that she intends some mischief towards Rebecca. Now, Captain Bryce, I tell you frankly that I want you to act as guardian angel to my sister for a week."

Jack laughed.

"That's a very delightful task," he said politely. "When do I start?"

"Tomorrow – no, make it the following day," said Sittingborn. "The fees – "

"You can arrange those with Mr Hemmer," said Jack.

Half an hour later he left the house, and brother and sister exchanged smiling glances.

"Well, 'Becca, I think I have got him," remarked Sittingborn. "What do you think of him?"

The girl shrugged.

"He's all right," she said indifferently; "but I hate these big men. They've always such a good opinion of themselves. Joe," she went on suddenly, "I don't want anything to happen on Tuesday night. I've promised to go to the theatre with Felix Monstein, and Felix is so jealous and so suspicious that if I broke off that engagement" – she shrugged – "he might break another, and I can't afford to lose him now I've got him hooked."

In this inelegant language did Miss Rebecca Sittingborn reveal her own ambition.

Sittingborn nodded. It was just as serious a matter for him that his sister's engagement to one of the richest men in the City should not be jeopardized.

"That can be fixed," he declared confidently, "even if it comes off before Tuesday. Anyway, there is no reason why you shouldn't go if you have a box."

"You're a dear," said the girl, kissing him with a loud smack, and Mr Sittingborn smiled complacently.

On the appointed day Jack called and was shown into the drawing-room, where Rebecca was waiting for him. His duties, he learnt, were to look after the girl during the daytime, her brother arranging for her care in the evening. Though she might not like big men, she found Jack a very good and sympathetic listener. He learnt, incidentally, of her engagement to Felix Monstein, and noted that fact for future reference. He had a trick of drawing out the confidence of people, and he had not been with her four hours before he was acquainted, not only with the fact of her engagement, but with the eccentricities of the jealous Mr Monstein.

"He hates me to be seen with anybody else," she said. "In fact, I think if he knew you were here he'd have a fit, and I should be sending my engagement ring back tomorrow."

She looked at the bunch of diamonds on her finger, and added: "Not that I should send back two thousand pounds' worth of brilliants without a little thought."

On the third day of his guardianship, that being a Monday, Jack Bryce had gone home to puzzle out the why and wherefore of his engagement, and was sitting before his fire, smoking his pipe, when the telephone bell rang, and the agitated voice of Mr Sittingborn greeted him.

"She's gone, Bryce," he wailed.

"Gone? Who?" asked Jack.

"My sister. She disappeared from the house an hour ago, accompanied by two veiled women."

"I'll come round," said Jack, and hung up the receiver.

He dressed quickly, found a cab, and was at Grosvenor Place in a quarter of an hour. He found Mr Sittingborn pacing up and down the drawing-room with appropriate expressions of misery upon his face.

He had nothing further to add to the information he had already given save that he was certain that Rebecca had been kidnapped by Madame Vashti.

"She has a house on Wimbledon Common," he explained, "and I am pretty certain that my sister is there."

"Why not inform the police?" asked Jack.

"There are many reasons," said Sittingborn sharply; "and if I wanted to make this a police job I shouldn't have employed you."

"That's logical," admitted Jack. "What do you want me to do?"

"I want you to get her away, Bryce. Go down to Wimbledon and have a good look at the house. Happily, the architect is a friend of mine, and tomorrow, if nothing has happened in the meantime, I will get you plans of the building, and we shall have to consider taking more drastic steps."

Jack went to Wimbledon in the man's car, and Mr Sittingborn accompanied him. The house was a beautiful erection in the Georgian style, facing Wimbledon Common, and certainly did not have the appearance of hiding any sinister secret, for the windows were lit up, and carriages and cars were coming and going.

"I know she's got a party tonight," said Sittingborn in a low voice, "but that's probably a blind."

"Shall I go in and see Madame Vashti?"

"No, no, no," exclaimed the other quickly. "You'd just put her on her guard. Oh, my poor Rebecca!"

"I think it would be pretty easy to get into the house," remarked Jack, looking at the building with the eye of a professional burglar. "But, on the whole, it would be better if we got the plans first."

"I agree," said Mr Sittingborn hurriedly, and they drove back to town.

The next morning Jack called at Grosvenor Place and found that his employer had succeeded in his scheme to secure the plans.

"I'm pretty certain she's confined in this place," said Sittingborn, solemnly tapping the paper with his finger; "and here is the very room. You see, it is away from the house, and is approached by this passage."

"A second-storey room," said Jack, examining the plans. "And it has a window. Do you know whether it is barred?"

"No; it is not barred," replied the other eagerly. "Now, let me give you my suggestions."

He closed the door, and assumed a more confidential tone.

"I know Madame Vashti and her ways. She goes to bed very early, unless she has a party on. Her servants are mostly old people, and there is nothing like a watch kept in spite of the fact that she has a lot of valuable property in the house. I have been on the telephone this morning to some friends of mine, and we can get you the necessary implements to make an entrance into the house."

"Like what?" asked Jack cautiously.

"Well, I can get you a telescopic ladder, and that'll be useful. I can get you a jemmy and a small centre-bit – so small that you can carry it in your waistcoat pocket."

He expected some objections from Wireless Bryce, and was surprised and secretly glad when Jack, with an unexpected eagerness, accepted the scheme without demur.

Jack spent the whole of the day pursuing inquiries, and at night he made a final call at Grosvenor Place to collect the implements which his employer had procured.

"There is no news of your sister, I suppose?"

"None whatever," replied the other gloomily. "You can't imagine how anxious I am."

85

"Oh, yes, I can," said Jack.

He took up the portable ladder and balanced it in his hand. It was a beautifully constructed apparatus, and when folded it went easily into the golf bag which Mr Sittingborn, with admirable forethought, had provided for its carriage.

"There is only one point I want to make," said Jack, "and that is that you will give me a written paper" – Mr Sittingborn's face fell – "instructing your sister to go with me. She may doubt my *bona fides*, even though she knows I am engaged in this work."

"With the greatest pleasure," said Sittingborn, relieved. He had expected that Jack was asking for a note in which the object of this attempted rescue was put down in black and white.

He went to his desk and wrote:

DEAR REBECCA,
I want you to go with Captain Bryce wherever he wishes tonight.

and signed it with his name.

"You see," explained Jack, "it may not be possible or expedient to come straight back to Grosvenor Place. I may want to take her out of London, or they may be so hot on my track that I have to go just where I can; and if your sister raised any objection, that, of course, would be fatal."

"I quite see," said the other heartily, and offered his hand. "I wish you good luck."

He waited till Jack was gone, then dressed quickly. His car was waiting in the mews at the back of the house, and in five minutes he was on his way to Richmond.

Madame Vashti, so far from being young and pretty, was middle-aged and stout, and she greeted Mr Sittingborn warmly.

"Well, this is a sight for sore eyes, Joe," she said. "I didn't expect you."

They were evidently the best of friends, as well they might be, because Madame Vashti was Sittingborn's sister.

"What brought you down here?" she asked as he seated himself.

"Well, I've every reason to believe there's going to be a burglary committed in your house tonight."

Madame Vashti showed her white teeth in a broad smile.

"They'll have a job," she said grimly. "Since that last attempt I've always had a night watchman patrolling the house after we've gone to bed, and the rubies are safe enough in the strong-room. I must show you a new one I've got from Burma, Joe."

"Wait a moment," he said. "I want your watchman to make himself scarce, and I'd like you to keep all the lights out."

"The lights in the corridors, you mean?" she asked in surprise, and Mr Sittingborn nodded.

"You don't want to scare them, eh?" she nodded thoughtfully. "Well, I can arrange that. But what are you going to do with these people?"

"There will only be one," said Sittingborn confidently, "and he will come at a quarter past twelve."

He chuckled.

"What's the joke?" asked the woman.

"A little joke of mine," said Sittingborn. "Now I must be off, Jenny. I'm going down to the police station, and you needn't worry, because I shall be on hand to pinch our friend. And I think that when we've caught him with burglar's tools in his possession, he'll have a little difficulty in explaining them away, and I shall get one back on the dirty trick he played on me."

His sister looked mystified.

"One of your little tricks, is it?" she remarked admiringly. "Well, you know your own business best, and I won't attempt to pry."

At eleven o'clock that night, accompanied by three officers of the law, Mr Sittingborn took his place in a very cold and draughty shrubbery, waiting for the appearance of the man whom he had good reason to hate. Half-past eleven chimed from the neighbouring church, then the third quarter, and finally midnight.

"I've got an idea he'll be along pretty soon," whispered Sittingborn to the detective at his side.

"Where did you get to hear of this, sir?" asked that officer curiously.

"I get to know a lot of things," said the complacent Mr Sittingborn, and with this cryptic reply the policeman had to be satisfied.

The quarter after struck, and still there was no sign of Jack. The bells chimed the half-hour after midnight, and the quarter to one, and finally one, and still there was no sign of a burglar.

Sittingborn was beside himself with rage. What had scared Bryce, he wondered?

At half-past two the police officers suggested that they should leave one man on guard, and the rest of them should go home to bed.

"I'm afraid you've been hoaxed, Mr Sittingborn," said the inspector.

Sittingborn did not reply. He flung himself into his car, and was driven rapidly back to London. Something had occurred to frighten Bryce, he supposed, and cheered up as he thought that the attempt need only be postponed.

He reached Grosvenor Place a little after three, and let himself in with his key. There were lights in the drawing-room, which fact was very surprising. For Mr Sittingborn, like many other rich men, was extremely economical. He opened the door and stepped in, then gasped his surprise. For Rebecca was sitting on the divan, her face in her hands, and she had evidently been weeping. She raised a tear-stained face to his, and there was something besides sorrow in her red eyes.

"So you've come back, have you?" she said with a dangerous calm. "Well, you've made a nice mess of things!"

"What have I done?" demanded the innocent Sittingborn.

"What have you done?" repeated the girl scornfully. "Why, my engagement with Monstein is off, that's all. I've had a fearful row with him, and he's sent back all my letters by special messenger, and asked for his ring. I hope he may get it," she concluded viciously.

The man sank down in a chair, his mouth open.

"Your engagement is off?" he cried incredulously.

"Of course it's off!" she snapped. "You must have known that he wouldn't stand that. But, like a fool, I thought it was one of your clever plans, and that everything would come right. I thought you had told Monstein, and he had agreed!"

"Look here," shouted the bewildered Sittingborn, "I don't know what on earth you're talking about. Agreed to what?"

"Didn't you send that fellow Bryce to me tonight?"

"Send Bryce to you?" said the man in a strangled voice. "No!"

"Well, he came," went on the girl bitterly. "All dressed up for the dance, so to speak. I was surprised to see him; I didn't imagine he knew that I was staying with Aunt Mary at Hampstead."

Mr Sittingborn said nothing, and then in a hollow voice: "He must have shadowed me all day, the swine!"

"Well, anyway, he came about eight o'clock," said the girl impatiently. "Just as I was dressed ready to go to the Gaiety to meet Felix. And he told me that he had orders to go with me. I told him how impossible it was, that I already had an engagement at the theatre, but he produced seats for two stalls, and said everything was all right."

"And you went with him?"

The girl nodded.

"We sat in the stalls, and there was Monstein sitting in the box, positively glaring down at me. I thought it was some new scheme, some change of plan of yours, but I was mighty uncomfortable, and when I met Monstein in the lobby after the show he treated me like dirt," she wailed.

A light began to dawn upon Mr Sittingborn's brain.

"Did you tell this" – he found a difficulty in finding a word – "this man Bryce that Monny was jealous, and that you had an engagement to go to the theatre with him?"

"Yes," sobbed the girl.

"Then you're the fool," snarled the other. "I see it now; he's tumbled to our scheme, and the dog thought out a good way of punishing me. I'll see Bryce tomorrow," he said with determination.

He saw Bryce in his lodgings, and Captain Bryce greeted him as a friend.

"None of that," said Sittingborn roughly. "You've played a low trick on me, Bryce, and I'm going to make you pay for it."

"I'm going to make you pay something, too," said Bryce, and handed the other a bill.

Mr Sittingborn took it mechanically. He read:

To three days' guardianship – 12 guineas; to rescuing Miss Sittingborn from a fate worse than death – 100 guineas.

"What do you mean?" asked Sittingborn. "Rescuing her 'from a fate worse than death'? Why, dash it, you took her to a theatre!"

"And rescued her from that insufferable bounder, Monstein," said Jack gently. "And really, Sittingborn, it was worth the money."

THE CASE OF AN HEIRESS

Much of Messrs. Hemmer & Hemmer's practice was at the Chancery Bar. They had to do with heirs and heiresses whom they had never heard about or seen, though the person who left them money and property might be very well known to them, and occasionally it happened that they discovered themselves acting for a client with whom ordinarily they would never have done business.

Miss Lizzie Colbert was such a legatee. She had been left £6,000 by an uncle who was a client of Hemmer & Hemmer, and that £6,000 must have seemed to her a very great fortune, for she was employed in a firm of City drapers behind the counter at a moderate wage.

The sudden acquisition of wealth will often turn the most generous and prodigal spirits into paths of economy, if not meanness. Similarly, it makes spendthrifts of those who heretofore have conserved their slender resources with a rigorous hand.

Miss Colbert had been a modest, diffident, and pretty girl, who would not have said "boo" to a goose until her good fortune arrived. Until then she had trusted all people, and had faith in humanity. But after she became the possessor of wealth she took a view, which is not uncommon, that the whole world was conspiring to rob her, and that the leader of these brigands was the eminent firm of lawyers, Messrs. Hemmer & Hemmer.

"I don't mind that so much," said Mr Hemmer, relating his grievances to Captain Jack Bryce. "Indeed, it would be a very safe attitude to adopt if she did not make exceptions."

"Has she found an exception?" asked Jack.

"Yes, she has," nodded Hemmer. "There is a smart young clerk employed by the firm she works for, who looks like participating very largely in her good fortune. She came up to me today, and told me just how she's going to turn that six thousand into twenty thousand in under a year, and when she had related this fact I knew that there was a clever man somewhere in the background, and by judicious inquiries I discovered that Mr Tennyson – who's no relation to the poet of that name – is the bright genius who is going to perform this financial miracle."

"Do you want me to do anything?" asked Jack. The other threw out his hands with a gesture of despair.

"I don't see exactly what you can do unless you take Mr Tennyson and drown him. Not," he added hastily, "that I suggest anything so unlawful."

"What is the girl's particular illusion?"

"The infallibility of Tennyson, I think," said Mr Hemmer dryly. "At any rate, this young man has got a great scheme for floating a motor-car repair factory which requires exactly the amount of capital the girl possesses. She is wildly enthusiastic, and came up here to ask me to sell all the gilt-edged stocks I had bought for her, and transfer them to her account. She was going to be the secretary in the company at a salary of a thousand a year, and she pointed out that in six years she will not only have recovered her capital outlay, but will also have participated in the enormous profits which this motor-car repairing factory will make for her."

Jack's grimace was eloquent.

"Of course, she'll lose every bean. Are you carrying out her wishes?"

"I must," said Mr Hemmer. "I have no authority to stop her making a fool of herself. But I'm rather sorry, because she's quite a nice little thing, and really deserves better treatment than she's going to get at the hands of Mr Harold Tennyson."

"I'll see Mr Harold Tennyson," declared Jack after a moment's thought. "Can you give me his address?"

"I don't think you can do very much – but here's where he lives." The lawyer took a card from his table and scribbled a few words upon it. "I warn you, Bryce, that this fellow is a pretty shrewd man, and, from what the girl has told me, he is one of those amateur lawyers whom it is a ticklish business to monkey with."

Jack sought Mr Tennyson, who occupied a little flat in Maida Vale, though it was not here that he found him. It appeared that Mr Tennyson had already begun operations, for he was discovered in a factory which had formerly been used for the making of war material, and he was directing and superintending the painting of its interior with great enthusiasm. He was a slight man, with black, curly hair, and a trim moustache, and that he was no fool Jack realized by his first words.

"You're from Hemmer & Hemmer, I suppose?" he asked with a broad smile. "Name of Bryce, isn't it?"

Jack was a little taken aback.

"Got me first shot," he said.

"I heard about you," went on Tennyson. "You're the gentleman who acts as private assassin to the firm." He laughed at his own jest. "Now, just let me tell you, Mr Captain Bryce," he added significantly, "that I know the law as well as your boss, and if you try any of those tricks on me you're going to get into serious trouble."

"Not half as serious as the trouble you'll be in," smiled Jack. "And, after that threat, going on the principle that one might as well be hung for a sheep as for a lamb, I'll deserve any punishment I get. But I've not come here to beat you up, Mr Tennyson, but to have a look round. Naturally, Mr Hemmer is anxious to know what prospects our client has of making the beautiful profits which you have promised."

He met the other's eye and held it for a moment.

"The profits will be made all right," said Mr Tennyson. "Would you like me to show you round?"

Jack expressed the desire, though he was less interested in the building than in the man.

"Of course you know that Miss Colbert and I are going to be married," remarked Tennyson as he led the way upstairs.

"I expected something like that," replied Jack. "But won't your wife object?"

The man swung round on him with a frown.

"My wife?" he snarled. "I'm not married. If you're under that impression you're barking up the wrong tree, Mr Clever."

"I don't think it," said Jack. "It just occurred to me. Men with black, curly hair and a glib tongue are usually married very early in life."

A reply which seemed to restore Mr Tennyson's good nature, for he laughed.

"I'm going to use this room," he explained, "for tyre repairs."

The room was a fairly large one. Jack thought it was a little close, and mentioned the fact.

"Yes, the ventilation here is very bad, though I am going to have that seen to," said Tennyson easily. "Of course, one has not been able to incur the expenses that one would like, owing to the difficulty of getting your people to part with my young lady's money."

"No electric light here, either," commented Jack, looking down at the gas brackets.

"No, only gas," said the other; "but that'll be seen to when our ship comes home."

Jack looked round the room, from the tiny gas fire which was burning at one end, along the closed windows, and back to the door. The room was entirely void of any furniture, and had evidently been recently swept. A voice below had called them, and Tennyson turned to Jack with a grin.

"You'll be able to meet my fiancée," he said. "And perhaps that will set your mind at rest."

"My mind is never troubled," Jack reassured him. "But anything you can do to increase the equanimity will be very welcome."

At the foot of the stairs he met Mr Hemmer's client – a little girl with a weak face, who gave her fiancé such a look of adoration that Jack could have laughed but for the tragedy of it. She had brought some tea for the "Managing Director," and apparently brought it every afternoon. This she spread on the one table which the factory possessed with her own fair hands, and to the repast Jack was invited.

"Mr Hemmer hasn't been very kind," said the girl; "but, naturally, he can't know Harold as well as I do."

"But surely Mr Hemmer has advanced you money for all this?" Jack waved his hand to the painters at work at the far end of the shop.

"Harold has paid for it out of his own pocket, haven't you, dear?"

"I thought it would help you," said Harold modestly, and Jack's eyes twinkled.

He learnt later that the work had been going on for less than a week, that the painters and other workmen had not yet been paid, and that only a deposit had been lodged at the house agents from whom the factory had been hired; so that Harold's capital expenditure had been very little.

"I shall have my own money tomorrow," said the girl. "And do you know what I'm going to do, Harold darling? The moment my money is in the bank I'm going to give you a cheque for six thousand pounds."

"My dear, that's very sweet of you," murmured Harold; "but I think we can trust one another."

Later in the afternoon Jack reported to Hemmer.

"It's a bad case with these people," he said. "The man is a slippery customer, and is probably a crook."

Hemmer sighed.

"I've sent her my cheque," he said. "I got the brokers' account today, and there was nothing else for me to do."

"For how much is it?"

"It's a trifle over six thousand pounds. Some of the stocks I bought have appreciated in value."

The next afternoon Jack saw Mr Harold Tennyson again, and saw him by accident. He caught just a glimpse of his neat figure and his coat tails as he turned into a tourist agent in Ludgate Circus. Jack stopped in his stride. After a moment's hesitation he pushed open the big doors and went in after him. There was a crowd at the two big counters, and it was some time before the wireless man could see his quarry. Then he saw Mr Tennyson bent over the counter in earnest confabulation with a clerk, and from the fact that the clerk was examining books and jotting down notes, Jack gathered that Mr Tennyson was planning a route. He edged closer to the man; he could do this because there were two or three people waiting to attract the clerk's attention, and he saw a book of tickets being prepared and punched.

"To the Continent," noted Jack mentally, "and only one ticket. I wonder when he's going?"

That doubt was set at rest when the clerk looked up from his writing-pad and asked: "Will you go on the evening of the eighth or the morning of the ninth?"

"The eighth," said Mr Tennyson, and Jack melted into the crowd, and was interested in another department when Tennyson turned away from the counter and left the agency.

Tennyson was going to the Continent on Saturday, and he was going alone. Jack frowned. Of course, there might be a very simple explanation for this visit abroad. Mr Tennyson might be going to buy machinery for his new business; but in that case he would at least make a stop at Paris, and by the number of tickets which had been punched together in the folder it was clear that he was going beyond Paris.

He made it his business to go again to the factory, and chose the tea hour. It seemed to him that he was not so very welcome, for the girl was cold – was even brusque. Mr Tennyson, however, was politeness itself.

"Well," he asked jovially, "have you come to see what progress we've made? Sit down and have a cup of tea, Mr Bryce."

"You're doing splendidly," said Jack. "But, really, my business today was not so much to congratulate you upon the rapidity of your preparation as to put an idea in your way. A friend of mine," he lied glibly, "has a new vulcanizing machine, and I wondered whether you would care to come over to Wembley next Sunday and give me your opinion of it."

"It might be very useful to you, Harold," remarked the girl, interested. "Why don't you go?"

Mr Tennyson shook his head with a smile.

"Very sorry," he said, "but I've got to go to Manchester on Saturday evening to see about establishing an agency."

"When do you return?" demanded Jack. This, he knew, was the crucial question, and if the man failed to reply satisfactorily he was condemned. But to Jack's surprise it was the girl who answered.

"On Monday, of course," she replied with a smile. "You're taking me to the Promenade Concert on Monday, aren't you, Harold?"

"Yes, my dear, I shall be back by the afternoon train," agreed the man quickly.

Jack had learned all he wanted to know. The man had bought a ticket for either Italy or Austria, for Jack had recognized, amongst those that had been put up in the folder for him, the pink slips which carry a passenger across the Swiss Federal Railways. Therefore it was impossible that he could be back on Monday, and equally certain that he was deliberately deceiving the girl.

"Have you had your cheque from Mr Hemmer, Miss Colbert?" he asked politely, and the girl nodded.

"I'm getting it cleared, because my bank manager does not like letting me have so large a sum until the other cheque has been honoured."

"Then you're going to draw it all out at once, are you?" said Jack pleasantly.

"I told you – and I've told Mr Hemmer, too – what I'm going to do. I'm going to give the whole of it to dear Harold – I'll post you the cheque tonight, dear. You know I shan't see you tomorrow. I'm going to Hastings to stay with my cousin over the weekend."

"Bless you," said Mr Tennyson; and whether it was for the honour she was conferring upon her cousin or for the anticipated cheque, he did not explain.

"And I shall send it here, dear," she resumed softly. "Won't that be splendid? To our new office. Have you seen the fine painting over the door?"

"I've noticed it," said Jack.

"That will be all right," nodded Harold. "I'm in my little office here at nine o'clock every morning, and sometimes earlier."

"Good news!" remarked Jack ironically, but he did not give his cynicism too violent expression.

If Mr Tennyson was an early arrival next morning, much earlier was Captain Jack Bryce, who stationed himself at the end of the road where the new motor-repairing factory vaunted its existence in letters a foot long, and from that point he watched the postman make his first delivery, and ten minutes later the arrival of the brisk young man.

Another thing he noticed was that the workmen whom one usually expects to see arrive, did not put in an appearance. He found that Mr Harold Tennyson had paid them off on the previous night. The absence of workmen was all to the good, thought Jack as he walked slowly across to the tiny factory. The outer door was closed and locked, and he had to ring a bell and wait some time before Mr Tennyson made his appearance. That worthy was less genial and more surprised at such an early visitation.

"Hullo," he said ungraciously, "what do you want?"

"Just a little chat with you," said Jack, closing the door behind him. "You know the old saying," he said, as he locked the door and pushed the wrathful Harold before him into the rough and untidy office he had found for himself, "the early bird catches the worm, and I think I have caught you."

"Now, look here, Bryce; I've told you before that you'll get no change out of me if you try any of your violence. Understand once and for all that I have the law on my side and I'll not hesitate to employ it. I've got a clean record," he went on, emphasizing every word, "and I'm a respectable citizen and a ratepayer, amongst other things, and you've got no pull over me. I might tell you that you are committing a misdemeanour within the meaning of the law."

"And soon I shall be committing a felony," said Jack coolly. "You haven't a large correspondence, Harold."

"Don't call me Harold," snapped the man.

"I rather like the name of Harold, though I don't for one moment imagine it is your name. I should say Karl was nearer." By the quick movement of the man's eyes he guessed he was on the verge of a discovery. "Hungarian, of course," he said, as it came to him in a flash. "I ought to have associated those soulful eyes and coal-black hair with a fiddle – I suppose you play a fiddle?"

"There's no harm in being Hungarian," said the man sulkily. "Live and let live is my motto."

"Which means that other people can live as they can, so long as you can live as you like, eh?" went on Jack. "Now pass over that letter you received from the confiding Miss Colbert this morning."

"I'll do nothing of the kind," shouted the man, and tried to wrench himself from the other's grip. But he might as well have tried to push a house down. He felt a firm thumb under his chin, and his head was thrust back until it seemed that his neck would break, and then, with a yell, he thrust his hand into his pocket and produced the letter.

"Thank you," said Jack, "for your great and loving kindness and exceeding courtesy."

The letter had been opened, and he took out the cheque.

"Six thousand one hundred and fifty pounds," he remarked. "Quite a nest-egg. And I see it is an open cheque, made payable to bearer."

"If you touch that cheque or destroy it in any way," said the man with quiet malice, "whether I am Hungarian or not, you're going to get into serious trouble. That is my property, and it is a felony to destroy it."

"It is, indeed," said Jack, "and I'm not going to destroy it, believe me. But you are," he added significantly. "Though, after all, it doesn't matter" – he looked the other straight in the eye – "if it is destroyed. You can get another from Miss Colbert on Monday morning, can't you?"

The man made no reply.

"Unless of course, you contemplate slipping to the Continent tonight," continued Jack.

"What do you mean?" snarled the man.

"I mean this – that you have got tickets to take you to Hungary, and that you intend leaving by the night train, and presumably by way of Havre for your native land. Correct me, if I'm wrong. And you are taking with you six thousand one hundred and fifty pounds – which a foolish and loving woman has given to you. And in Hungary, at the present rate of exchange, you will be living, I daresay, like a prince by this time next week."

He looked at the cheque again.

"The South British Bank," he mused. "Well, that's fortunate. I suppose you know it is a peculiarity of the South British Bank that they never honour a cheque if so much as the corner is cut off accidentally, or if it is damaged in any way?"

"I don't know what you mean," said the man, his curiosity getting the better of his fear.

"You will soon learn," replied Jack, and, gripping him by the arm, he took him out of the office and up the stairs into the room above which he had inspected a few days previously. He closed the door behind him and locked it; then he walked round the room; testing the windows. They were made of thick, toughened glass. He stooped at the gas fire at one end of the room, lit a match, and set it burning. Then he took a small pair of pincers, which he had brought with him – for he had thought out his plans with great thoroughness – and, going to a gas bracket at the further end of the room, he nipped away the little handle by which the gas was turned on and off. Then he turned to the man.

"Take off your clothes," he said.

"Why?" demanded the other. "Curse you, I won't do it! You'll suffer for this! I'll have you for felony."

"Take off your clothes," said Jack quietly, "and save me the unpleasant task of stripping them from you. You can reduce yourself to your shirt and your underclothes. Take them off," he said sharply, making a threatening gesture, and the man slunk back with a cry.

With trembling fingers he obeyed. Coat and vest, trousers and boots were discarded, and Jack inspected him approvingly.

"Here is the cheque," he said, and to Harold's astonishment he handed him the small pink slip of paper.

He took the man's clothes and threw them outside the door; then he walked to the gas bracket near the window farthest from the fire, and with a deft turn of his pliers switched on the gas.

"There isn't much ventilation in this room," he drawled, "and there is only one chance of your escaping asphyxiation. It is to light that gas with the cheque. I have seen that there is nothing else burnable in the room."

"I don't see what you mean," said the man, dazed.

"I mean," repeated Jack patiently, "that you can either let the gas escape and eventually overcome you, or cause an explosion, because there's a fire burning at the other end; or you can use your cheque as a pipelighter, and I think it doesn't matter which end you burn, because the figure is at one end and the signature at the other. I calculate that either will be burnt by the time you can carry your light from the fire to the gas bracket. Do you get my meaning?"

"I'll not burn it! I'll not burn it!" screamed the man.

"Then in about one hour, unless all our views on theology are mistaken," said Jack, "you'll be doing a little burning yourself."

And he went out, slamming the door behind him.

He walked carelessly into the road and looked up at the windows of the room, and after ten minutes he saw a light burning near the window and grinned. Then, taking the key, he flung it with all his force at the window and saw it smash, and heard the tinkle as it dropped in the room; then he went to his lunch with a good appetite.

That night he interviewed Miss Colbert in the midst of her impressed relations, and told her a few home truths about Harold Tennyson, Esquire.

"I can't believe it," declared the girl. "I must have it from his own lips."

"I doubt if you will ever see him again," said Jack. And so it proved.

THE BEAUTIFUL MISS M'GREGGOR

Captain Jack Bryce was not particularly susceptible to feminine charms, and less impressed by beauty of countenance and carriage than most men. But he stood dumbfounded in the doorway of Mr Hemmer's private office, bereft of speech and movement, at the sight of the girl who sat opposite the old lawyer.

Mr Hemmer watched his embarrassment with a queer smile. As for the girl, she seemed in no wise disconcerted, nor yet impressed by his frank admiration.

"This is Miss M'Greggor – Captain Bryce, and you've come at an opportune moment, because Miss M'Greggor is in very serious trouble."

And then the eyes of the man and the girl met, and he experienced a queer little thrill like nothing he had ever known before. And she for the first time lost countenance and flushed a little.

"Mr Hemmer," she said, turning to the lawyer, "I know that my beauty is fatal, but I did not expect to produce such an effect in your office."

She spoke without vanity, without affectation, and immediately explained her attitude.

"You think I am very immodest, Captain Bryce, don't you?" she said with a twinkle in her eye. "But then, you see, I do not even pretend to have such bad taste that I can depreciate my own prettiness."

She made a wry little face.

"And if you can find any nice, homely girl who would like to exchange faces with me, Captain Bryce, I should be most happy if you would produce her and the magician who is capable of effecting the transfer."

It was Jack's turn to laugh.

"The truth is," explained Mr Hemmer, "that Miss M'Greggor's attractions have landed her into very serious trouble. Miss M'Greggor is the daughter of an old client of mine, and I am willing to go very far to give her the assistance she requires."

Jack mentally resolved that he would go even farther for one kindly look from those soft, grey eyes.

"Miss M'Greggor has just arrived from the Continent by the morning train," went on Hemmer, "and was telling me her story when you came in. Do you mind beginning again?"

She made a little face.

"It's not a nice story, Captain Bryce," she said, "and it concerns my good appearance, for which I am no more responsible, for which, therefore, I can take no greater pride, than you can for the hair on your head, or for your nicely shaped fingernails."

Jack put his hands in his pockets with a blush, and she laughed softly, but became serious immediately.

"I have been in Paris studying art," she continued, "and whilst I was there I made the acquaintance of M. Albert Ledroux, who is well known in Paris as a man about town, and a very gay young man about town, too. His father is one of the most powerful financiers in Europe, and possesses a great deal of influence. The Ledroux are known everywhere for their ruthless financial methods, and I am told that they stick at nothing to achieve their ends. Of course, that is only a manner of speaking, and may mean nothing definite, but I certainly know that neither Albert nor his father have very many scruples.

"I got to know Albert through some mutual friends, and I dined at their house in the Place d'Etoile, and spent a weekend with M. and Madame Ledroux at their château in Compiègne. Of course, Albert was in love with me, all the young men were – I'm really not being conceited, I am merely stating a very annoying fact – and if I had wished, I could have been Madame Ledroux, junior, with an unlimited bank balance and the responsibilities of an erratic husband.

"I did not choose," she concluded shortly. "Albert was not the type of man I admire by any means."

There was a moment's pause, then Miss M'Greggor resumed: "He was unattractive in many ways, and the long and the short of it is, that when he proposed to me I rejected him. I think I must have hurt his vanity very badly indeed, because he told me that I was the first woman he had ever proposed marriage to, and boasted of the ease with which he could accomplish his conquests. Old Ledroux was just as angry as his son, and came to see me at my little flat, and simply stormed at me. I was warned by some very good friends that young Ledroux was dangerous, and one of them, who knew something of his methods, insisted upon my carrying a little revolver, and, though I was very scornful at the idea that I needed any other protection than my own sense of righteousness, I carried this wretched little thing to oblige her."

She took from her handbag a tiny, silver-plated revolver with an ivory handle and laid it on the desk with a little shudder.

"Well, nothing happened for a week or two, and then I met Albert by chance – I think now that it wasn't so much a chance as a design carefully engineered by him – at a dinner party. He asked me to forgive him for the wild words he had spoken, and asked me to remain friends with him, and to this request I was only too anxious to agree. A few days later I saw him again. He brought a letter, apparently from Madame Ledroux, asking me if I would stay a weekend with them at their château in Brittany, and being anxious not to make bad blood or to continue antagonistic, I accepted."

She paused again, and knit her brows in thought.

"Of course, I ought to have known," she said, "but I had such confidence in myself that I didn't bother to make inquiries. The long and the short of it was that I arrived at the château in Brittany and found that I was the only guest, that Madame and M. Ledroux, senior, were not staying there, and that I was practically alone in the house with Albert. I was trapped in a locked room, the key of which was in

Albert's pocket. On the table lay two big diamond bangles, which he had brought with him. I insisted on leaving the house at once. He refused to open the door, and I struck him across the face. He lost his temper, and became violent. I was helpless against him, and had exhausted myself in the struggle when I remembered the pistol in my handbag, which was hanging on the back of my chair.

"I broke away from him, pulled the pistol out – and shot him."

"Dead?" inquired Jack, raising his eyebrows.

"No, he wasn't dead, but he was unconscious when I took the key from him. I went out, locking the door behind me. He had sent the servants away, but a chauffeur was still in the garage, and I told him that it was M. Ledroux's order that he should take me to Dieppe, which was only about twenty-five miles away. I got there just in time to catch the boat – and here I am."

There was a silence.

"Well, there's no danger for you, and they cannot extradite you, Miss M'Greggor."

"Ledroux can do anything," she said quietly.

"He can't upset the laws of this country," declared Mr Hemmer. "You cannot be extradited for a crime which you committed in France. If you were in France you could, of course, be arrested."

She shivered.

"I think I know what would be my fate," she said in a low voice. "The Ledroux are so powerful that I would never see the outside of a prison again. I tell you, Mr Hemmer, I'm frightened, frightened of what Ledroux and his agents will do in the next fortnight."

"Well, you needn't be frightened," smiled Hemmer. "Our friend here will look after you for that time and longer."

"For years, if necessary," said Jack fervently. Again the girl flushed, and looked with a kindly smile upon the tall, handsome man who had risen awkwardly, and now stood looking down at her with a face that was crimson.

"I hope not for so long," she replied. "I think they must take action in the next fortnight."

"Where are you staying, Miss M'Greggor?" asked Hemmer.

"With my sister at the Blickley Hotel, Baker Street," she replied. And it was to the Blickley Hotel the next morning that Jack reported himself for duty.

It was such a duty as he had never undertaken before. The days no sooner began than they had ended. He accompanied her on her shopping trips, and went with her once to Brighton. Her charm was irresistible, and he woke up one morning to the realization that for the first time in his life he was deeply and hopelessly in love.

Jack Bryce was a man in whom there was not one crooked streak. He called on the girl that morning, and was shown, as usual, into her sitting-room. She was alone. Her sister had just gone out to make some purchases, and, as usual, the girl greeted him with a look which set his heart fluttering.

"Miss M'Greggor, I've something to tell you."

She must have recognized the symptoms, for she stood back and regarded him gravely.

"I know I'm a lunatic, and I daresay you've met hundreds of lunatics before," he went on recklessly; "but I want to tell you something in plain language, lest, like a fool, I betray myself in other ways."

"You mean," she said slowly, when he paused, "that you think you are in love with me."

"I'm in love with you, all right," he corrected a little bitterly. "I have reached the age when love cannot be an illusion."

"You poor, dear old man," she mocked him. "I'm awfully sorry."

"I'm awfully sorry, too," he said in a voice more composed; "but I had to tell you this, and I do hope it is not going to make any difference to you. I swear to you that I will not bother you or annoy you in any way. Only I had to tell you."

She nodded.

"The fortnight is nearly up," he went on, "and the end of my guardianship is in sight. I don't know whether to be happy, or to be in despair."

"You ought to be happy," she said softly, "because that means the end of my danger."

"I wish it meant the end of mine," he remarked grimly.

She held out her hand to him.

"We're going to be good friends, aren't we? I know I'm not being as sympathetic as I ought; but, Captain Bryce, you've just fallen in love with my face, and you know nothing whatever about me. What you think is love will pass off, and whilst I don't think you will forget me, I believe I shall live with you only as a pleasant memory."

She had not taken her eyes from his face, and now she saw his despair. She shook her head.

"I know what you're thinking," she said. "You're wondering how you can convince me, and that is what they have all said."

A little pang of jealousy shot through his bosom, but he mastered it at once.

"I've never had a lover," she went on, half to herself; "I never found a man who could survive the test of my prettiness, and could convince me that it was something more than my appearance which attracted him."

"You're making it pretty hard," said Jack, keeping his voice steady with an effort. "Now let us forget that I ever spoke."

She was unusually quiet that day, and spoke very little to him, addressing herself mainly to her sister, a matronly woman of thirty-five, who had little of her relative's beauty.

Jack's duty ended at nine o'clock, when Molly retired to her rooms for the night, except on those evenings when she went to the theatre. This night she said goodbye a little earlier, and he went home to his lodgings a very unhappy man. He was in his room taking off his coat when he felt something in his pocket. He took out a little parcel, and remembered it was something which the girl had bought that afternoon, and which he had carried for her. She might want it in the morning, though the chances were that she would not. But he seized any excuse to see her again, and, putting on his coat, he went back to the hotel.

The hall porter beckoned him from his desk.

"Have you seen Mrs Slater?" – this was the name of the married sister – he asked.

"No," said Jack.

"Well, sir, she's gone to look for you. Her sister has been taken away."

"Taken away?" repeated Jack, aghast.

"Two gentlemen called for her," said the hall-porter, "and took her away in a cab. I think she's gone to Waterloo Station to catch the Continental train."

"What sort of gentlemen?" asked Jack quickly.

"Foreigners, they were, sir," he said, and hesitated. "You'll excuse my saying so, sir, but it seemed to me that by the way they were holding her arms the lady was under arrest."

"But French police officers cannot arrest an English subject," said Jack.

The porter shrugged his shoulders. He knew nothing about the niceties of international law.

Jack did not hesitate. He raced out of the hotel and called a taxi.

"Get me to Waterloo as quick as you can," he told the driver. "I'll give you a sovereign if you get me there before the mail goes."

"Can't do that, sir," said the man. "It goes" – he looked up at an illuminated clock – "it leaves in five minutes."

"Do your best," said Jack.

He got to the platform as the tail end of the Havre train went out. The ticket collector on the barrier remembered a very pretty lady going through. She was accompanied by two men who said they were police officers, and that the woman had been extradited.

"Were you thinking of going to Southampton, sir?" asked the man. "There's the train. It is only the first portion of the mail that has left. The second goes in a quarter of an hour. Have you got your ticket?"

Jack thought a moment.

"I have neither ticket nor passport," he replied; "but that lady has been kidnapped, and it is vitally necessary I should go. Can you get me a ticket?"

The inspector shook his head.

"Not without a passport, sir, although the regulations aren't so strict as they were."

"Get me a ticket! I won't attempt to land in France, I promise you," said Jack. "Here is a tenner for yourself, now do the best you can."

Five minutes before the second half of the boat train left the official came back with a ticket.

"Here's the tenner," he said; "I'll take your word, sir, that you're trying to do that lady a turn, and I'll give you that service for nothing."

And, try as hard as he could, Jack could not persuade the man to accept the bribe.

The Continental service that night was a particularly heavy one, and this fact explained why the train was running in two portions. He got to the dock station as the siren of the cross-Channel boat was sounding its last warning, though time enough was given for the passengers to get on board.

It was a rainy night, the decks were deserted. On his journey down Jack had decided that if these people had so carefully planned the abduction of the girl they would have engaged a cabin. He did not doubt what their object was. It was to secure her arrest the moment she touched the soil of France, where the influence of Ledroux was paramount.

So it was to the cabin list that he addressed himself, and a little talk with the purser acquainted him with the principal occupants.

"Two gentlemen and a lady? Yes, sir. There are two gentlemen and a lady in No. 17. That's the Imperial suite. A political prisoner, I think," he added, and looked suspiciously at Jack.

"That's all right," said Jack shamelessly. "I'm from Scotland Yard."

With this the officer seemed satisfied.

The Imperial suite he found. It had three windows looking on the main promenade deck, but these had been closed and shuttered. He listened, but could hear nothing, for the noise of the engines below, and the rush of water and rain made eavesdropping impossible. He had to wait some time before the alleyways were clear. The stewards were going in and out with refreshments, passengers were re-sorting their baggage, but presently there was a lull in this confusion, and just as the ship was rounding the Nab Lighthouse, he walked boldly to the door of the Imperial suite and turned the handle. The door was locked. He knocked gently, the diffident knock of a steward, and heard the key snapped back, and the door was opened a few inches.

"Excuse me," said Jack, and opened it still more, stepping into the stateroom and closing the door behind him.

There were two men, one evidently in a superior station of life, and the second a burly-looking individual, who had "ex-police officer" written all over him. At the sight of him they jumped up, but he had no eyes for them. He was looking at the girl who was sitting in an armchair, her hands clasped on her knees, her face white and drawn.

She did not realize he was in the room until one of the men uttered an exclamation, and then she raised her eyes slowly, and at sight of Jack her face went pink, then white again, and with one run she was by his side and his arm was round her.

Then the big man leapt at him. Jack put the girl quickly aside and turned. He was too late to avoid the blow, which struck him full in the face, but the next instant his hand was about the man's throat, and he had lifted him bodily and thrown him with a crash into the chair which the girl had occupied. Then he turned on the younger man, and this time realized he had a more dangerous opponent, for in the hands of Albert Ledroux, as he guessed him to be, was an automatic pistol, and that pistol was pointed straight at his heart.

"Put up your hands," ordered the young man between his teeth. He spoke in indifferent English.

Jack put his hands up obediently, and stepped back towards the wall. He was a tall man, and when his hands were raised they touched the ceiling of the cabin. They could touch also three little bottle-shaped fire extinguishers which hung in a rack on the wall behind him, and before Ledroux knew what had happened one of these was flying in his direction.

He turned his head just in time to miss it, but in that fraction of a second he lost his advantage, for Jack was on him, his wrist was turned, and he screamed at the intolerable agony of it, dropping his pistol on the ground.

"Now," remarked Jack, "I'm going to have a settlement with you people," and he spoke in French.

"You shall pay for this," breathed Ledroux, white with pain. "Remember we shall be in France in five hours, and then I shall have you."

"I shall be in France, mademoiselle will be in France, but you, my friend – where will you be? You and your companion will be at the bottom of the sea."

He picked up the pistol, and was balancing it in his hand.

"Come here, fat one," he said to the bigger of the two Frenchmen, and when the man obeyed he searched him deftly.

He found, as he had expected, a pair of handcuffs in the man's overcoat pocket, and these he snapped scientifically to the right wrist of Ledroux and the left of his companion.

There was a bedroom leading from this saloon. He opened the door and pushed them in.

"And now for the captain," he soliloquized, and, taking the girl's arm within his, he sought an interview with that individual.

The captain listened, and his face was grave. "This is a very serious business," he said, "but I cannot put back, and there will be an awful row when this thing is discovered on the other side. I mean what you have done to Ledroux."

"I don't think he'll bleat much about it," retorted Jack dryly. "It's a pretty serious offence against international law to attempt to kidnap a British subject."

The captain nodded.

"One thing is certain," he said seriously, "and that is that the moment you touch land, this lady will be arrested, because these people are certain to have agents waiting for them. I don't know what to do."

He fingered his beard thoughtfully.

"I'll tell you what I'll do," he declared, "I'll take this risk. We're rounding the Isle of Wight, and I'll bring the ship to Ventnor and stand in shore as close as I possibly can. I'll have a boat lowered, and you can row the young lady ashore."

It was two o'clock in the morning as Jack pulled steadily past the pier lights of Ventnor, and in the smoother water he rested on his oars, and looked back at the mail boat disappearing into the gloom. The girl who sat in the stern with the tiller lines in her hand failed to see his face in the darkness. Then dropping the lines, she came forward and sat by his side.

"We're safe now," she said.

"Yes, my dear, you're safe now," replied Jack.

She laughed.

"Your voice is quite sad," she reproached him. "Aren't you glad you've got me back? Or didn't you mean what you said to me this morning – no, it was yesterday morning – at the hotel?"

"I meant every word," said Jack huskily.

"Then I'll tell you something." She snuggled closer to him. "I don't want your guardianship to end this week. I want it to go on – permanently."

She said the last word in so low a voice that he had to stoop to hear her. In stooping his face came nearer to hers, and he kissed her.

"You're very beautiful," he whispered.

"You can't see my face." Her laugh was smothered against his coat.

"That proves that there is more beauty in you than is discernible to the eye," said Wireless Bryce, and at that moment the nose of his boat bumped on the pier steps.

EDGAR WALLACE

BIG FOOT

Footprints and a dead woman bring together Superintendent Minton and the amateur sleuth Mr Cardew. Who is the man in the shrubbery? Who is the singer of the haunting Moorish tune? Why is Hannah Shaw so determined to go to Pawsy, 'a dog lonely place' she had previously detested? Death lurks in the dark and someone must solve the mystery before BIG FOOT strikes again, in a yet more fiendish manner.

BONES IN LONDON

The new Managing Director of Schemes Ltd has an elegant London office and a theatrically dressed assistant – however, Bones, as he is better known, is bored. Luckily there is a slump in the shipping market and it is not long before Joe and Fred Pole pay Bones a visit. They are totally unprepared for Bones' unnerving style of doing business, unprepared for his unique style of innocent and endearing mischief.

EDGAR WALLACE

BONES OF THE RIVER

'Taking the little paper from the pigeon's leg, Hamilton saw it was from Sanders and marked URGENT. *Send Bones instantly to Lujamalababa… Arrest and bring to headquarters the witch doctor.*'

It is a time when the world's most powerful nations are vying for colonial honour, a time of trading steamers and tribal chiefs. In the mysterious African territories administered by Commissioner Sanders, Bones persistently manages to create his own unique style of innocent and endearing mischief.

THE DAFFODIL MYSTERY

When Mr Thomas Lyne, poet, poseur and owner of Lyne's Emporium insults a cashier, Odette Rider, she resigns. Having summoned detective Jack Tarling to investigate another employee, Mr Milburgh, Lyne now changes his plans. Tarling and his Chinese companion refuse to become involved. They pay a visit to Odette's flat and in the hall Tarling meets Sam, convicted felon and protégé of Lyne. Next morning Tarling discovers a body. The hands are crossed on the breast, adorned with a handful of daffodils.

EDGAR WALLACE

THE JOKER
(USA: THE COLOSSUS)

While the millionaire Stratford Harlow is in Princetown, not only does he meet with his lawyer Mr Ellenbury but he gets his first glimpse of the beautiful Aileen Rivers, niece of the actor and convicted felon Arthur Ingle. When Aileen is involved in a car accident on the Thames Embankment, the driver is James Carlton of Scotland Yard. Later that evening Carlton gets a call. It is Aileen. She needs help.

THE SQUARE EMERALD
(USA: THE GIRL FROM SCOTLAND YARD)

'Suicide on the left,' says Chief Inspector Coldwell pleasantly, as he and Leslie Maughan stride along the Thames Embankment during a brutally cold night. A gaunt figure is sprawled across the parapet. But Coldwell soon discovers that Peter Dawlish, fresh out of prison for forgery, is not considering suicide but murder. Coldwell suspects Druze as the intended victim. Maughan disagrees. If Druze dies, she says, 'It will be because he does not love children!'

OTHER TITLES BY EDGAR WALLACE AVAILABLE DIRECT
FROM HOUSE OF STRATUS

Quantity		£	$(US)	$(CAN)	€
	THE ADMIRABLE CARFEW	6.99	12.95	19.95	13.50
	THE ANGEL OF TERROR	6.99	12.95	19.95	13.50
	THE AVENGER *(USA: THE HAIRY ARM)*	6.99	12.95	19.95	13.50
	BARBARA ON HER OWN	6.99	12.95	19.95	13.50
	BIG FOOT	6.99	12.95	19.95	13.50
	THE BLACK ABBOT	6.99	12.95	19.95	13.50
	BONES	6.99	12.95	19.95	13.50
	BONES IN LONDON	6.99	12.95	19.95	13.50
	BONES OF THE RIVER	6.99	12.95	19.95	13.50
	THE CLUE OF THE NEW PIN	6.99	12.95	19.95	13.50
	THE CLUE OF THE SILVER KEY	6.99	12.95	19.95	13.50
	THE CLUE OF THE TWISTED CANDLE	6.99	12.95	19.95	13.50
	THE COAT OF ARMS				
	(USA: THE ARRANWAYS MYSTERY)	6.99	12.95	19.95	13.50
	THE COUNCIL OF JUSTICE	6.99	12.95	19.95	13.50
	THE CRIMSON CIRCLE	6.99	12.95	19.95	13.50
	THE DAFFODIL MYSTERY	6.99	12.95	19.95	13.50
	THE DARK EYES OF LONDON				
	(USA: THE CROAKERS)	6.99	12.95	19.95	13.50
	THE DAUGHTERS OF THE NIGHT	6.99	12.95	19.95	13.50
	A DEBT DISCHARGED	6.99	12.95	19.95	13.50
	THE DEVIL MAN	6.99	12.95	19.95	13.50
	THE DOOR WITH SEVEN LOCKS	6.99	12.95	19.95	13.50
	THE DUKE IN THE SUBURBS	6.99	12.95	19.95	13.50
	THE FACE IN THE NIGHT	6.99	12.95	19.95	13.50
	THE FEATHERED SERPENT	6.99	12.95	19.95	13.50
	THE FLYING SQUAD	6.99	12.95	19.95	13.50
	THE FORGER *(USA: THE CLEVER ONE)*	6.99	12.95	19.95	13.50
	THE FOUR JUST MEN	6.99	12.95	19.95	13.50
	FOUR SQUARE JANE	6.99	12.95	19.95	13.50

ALL HOUSE OF STRATUS BOOKS ARE AVAILABLE FROM GOOD BOOKSHOPS
OR DIRECT FROM THE PUBLISHER:

Internet:	**www.houseofstratus.com** including synopses and features.
Email:	**sales@houseofstratus.com**
	info@houseofstratus.com
	(please quote author, title and credit card details.)

OTHER TITLES BY EDGAR WALLACE AVAILABLE DIRECT
FROM HOUSE OF STRATUS

Quantity		£	$(US)	$(CAN)	€
☐	THE FOURTH PLAGUE	6.99	12.95	19.95	13.50
☐	THE FRIGHTENED LADY	6.99	12.95	19.95	13.50
☐	GOOD EVANS	6.99	12.95	19.95	13.50
☐	THE HAND OF POWER	6.99	12.95	19.95	13.50
☐	THE JOKER (USA: THE COLOSSUS)	6.99	12.95	19.95	13.50
☐	THE JUST MEN OF CORDOVA	6.99	12.95	19.95	13.50
☐	THE KEEPERS OF THE KING'S PEACE	6.99	12.95	19.95	13.50
☐	THE LAW OF THE FOUR JUST MEN	6.99	12.95	19.95	13.50
☐	THE LONE HOUSE MYSTERY	6.99	12.95	19.95	13.50
☐	THE MAN WHO BOUGHT LONDON	6.99	12.95	19.95	13.50
☐	THE MAN WHO KNEW	6.99	12.95	19.95	13.50
☐	THE MAN WHO WAS NOBODY	6.99	12.95	19.95	13.50
☐	THE MIND OF MR J G REEDER				
	(USA: THE MURDER BOOK OF J G REEDER)	6.99	12.95	19.95	13.50
☐	MORE EDUCATED EVANS	6.99	12.95	19.95	13.50
☐	MR J G REEDER RETURNS				
	(USA: MR REEDER RETURNS)	6.99	12.95	19.95	13.50
☐	MR JUSTICE MAXELL	6.99	12.95	19.95	13.50
☐	RED ACES	6.99	12.95	19.95	13.50
☐	ROOM 13	6.99	12.95	19.95	13.50
☐	SANDERS	6.99	12.95	19.95	13.50
☐	SANDERS OF THE RIVER	6.99	12.95	19.95	13.50
☐	THE SINISTER MAN	6.99	12.95	19.95	13.50
☐	THE SQUARE EMERALD				
	(USA: THE GIRL FROM SCOTLAND YARD)	6.99	12.95	19.95	13.50
☐	THE THREE JUST MEN	6.99	12.95	19.95	13.50
☐	THE THREE OAK MYSTERY	6.99	12.95	19.95	13.50
☐	THE TRAITOR'S GATE	6.99	12.95	19.95	13.50
☐	WHEN THE GANGS CAME TO LONDON	6.99	12.95	19.95	13.50

Tel: Order Line
       0800 169 1780 (UK)
        800 724 1100 (USA)
       International
       +44 (0) 1845 527700 (UK)
       +01   845 463 1100 (USA)

Fax: +44 (0) 1845 527711 (UK)
       +01   845 463 0018 (USA)
       (please quote author, title and credit card details.)

Send to: House of Stratus Sales Department
           Thirsk Industrial Park
           York Road, Thirsk
           North Yorkshire, YO7 3BX
           UK

PAYMENT

Please tick currency you wish to use:

☐ £ (Sterling)   ☐ $ (US)   ☐ $ (CAN)   ☐ € (Euros)

Allow for shipping costs charged per order plus an amount per book as set out in the tables below:

CURRENCY/DESTINATION

	£(Sterling)	$(US)	$(CAN)	€ (Euros)
Cost per order				
UK	1.50	2.25	3.50	2.50
Europe	3.00	4.50	6.75	5.00
North America	3.00	3.50	5.25	5.00
Rest of World	3.00	4.50	6.75	5.00
Additional cost per book				
UK	0.50	0.75	1.15	0.85
Europe	1.00	1.50	2.25	1.70
North America	1.00	1.00	1.50	1.70
Rest of World	1.50	2.25	3.50	3.00

PLEASE SEND CHEQUE OR INTERNATIONAL MONEY ORDER
payable to: HOUSE OF STRATUS LTD or HOUSE OF STRATUS INC. or card payment as indicated

STERLING EXAMPLE

Cost of book(s):..................... Example: 3 x books at £6.99 each: £20.97
Cost of order: .... Example: £1.50 (Delivery to UK address)
Additional cost per book:............... Example: 3 x £0.50: £1.50
Order total including shipping:.......... Example: £23.97

VISA, MASTERCARD, SWITCH, AMEX:

☐☐☐☐☐☐☐☐☐☐☐☐☐☐☐☐☐☐☐☐

Issue number (Switch only):

☐☐☐

Start Date: **Expiry Date:**

☐☐/☐☐   ☐☐/☐☐

Signature: _____

NAME: _____

ADDRESS: _____

COUNTRY: _____

ZIP/POSTCODE: _____

Please allow 28 days for delivery. Despatch normally within 48 hours.

Prices subject to change without notice.
Please tick box if you do not wish to receive any additional information. ☐

House of Stratus publishes many other titles in this genre; please check our website (**www.houseofstratus.com**) for more details.